HAUNTED HiJiNKS

MADISON JOHNS

HAUNTED HiJiNKS

AN AGNES BARTON PARANORMAL ROMANCE

BY

MADISON JOHNS

Sign up for my mystery newsletter list on Facebook
or visit http://madisonjohns.com.

Book cover:
www.coverkicks.com

Interior layout:
www.cohesionediting.com

NOTE FROM THE AUTHOR

I want to thank all of my readers, new and old, who have bought and continue to buy this series and love Agnes and Eleanor as much as I do. Writing about them is truly a labor of love, but I have wanted to do something much different, thus the subtitle, An Agnes Barton Paranormal Mystery. As always, please feel free to contact me anytime via my contact page on my website. I enjoy hearing from readers.

If not for you, I would not still be here, doing the one thing I love the most; writing.

CHAPTER ONE

Eleanor and I gathered our purses, rushing out the door. When we were settled in the car, Eleanor gushed, "I'm so excited. I can't believe the Butler Mansion will be turned into a bed and breakfast and that we were chosen to oversee preparations."

I massaged my brow thoughtfully. "You do know that we'll be working, right?"

"Yes, but it's not like we'll be pushing a broom." Eleanor gave me a concerned look. "Are you okay, Agnes? Maybe it's too soon for you to be out and about. I mean, since the accident you've not been yourself."

I cranked the engine over and tore off down US 23. I tried not to think about that day a few months back when I was sideswiped by an SUV as I was trying to avoid hitting a tourist who crossed on the green. They never even looked in my direction. Well, let's just say that the driver was as surprised as I was when my Mustang slid across his vehicle. We even locked eyes for a fraction of a second— that was before his side mirror flew off and grazed the side of my head through my open window. I was knocked out cold and didn't wake up for three whole days. And when I did come to, a muscular man with a full beard was sitting at my bedside at the hospital, among others. It took some prompting from my daughter, Martha before I remembered I even had a son. I guess that's what happens when you have a concussion. I can't remember exactly when the last time I'd seen Stuart was.

My fiancé, Andrew, was there, too, and my ever-faithful friend, Eleanor Mason. They told me my granddaughter, Sophia, had just left with my great-granddaughter, Andrea. All of this made sense to me. I had everyone around who loved me, but what I didn't understand was the ghostly apparition of a woman that also was there, and totally unseen by everyone else. At the time, I chocked it up to taking too many medications, but when everyone left and the gray shadowy figure remained, I hid under my covers for a while. Luckily, the next morning she was gone ... that was, until she showed up later that day. She kinda has a habit of appearing and disappearing, which is hard to get used to. Not that I could ever get used to seeing a ghost. My heart jumps a little every time and I can't help but wonder if I was injured more severely than Dr. Thomas had told me. I've pondered the how and why of the ghost's absences and wonder if she had ghostly business to take care of, because sure enough, she reappeared when I was released from the hospital later that week.

The glaring sunlight jarred me out of my deep thoughts and I stared in my rearview mirror, and sure enough, El and I had the same ghostly passenger parked in the backseat, one that only I could see. At least, Eleanor had never admitted to me that she'd seen a ghost. Eleanor's the type of person who would be scared to death at the prospect of seeing one. The ghost was quite slim and wore a quite-transparent green dress. Her bob-cut hairstyle was glowing about her head. As of yet, she hadn't spoken a word to me, which I'm eternally grateful for since I was already halfway ready for the loony bin, or so I had convinced myself.

I'm Agnes Barton, and I have been solving mysteries with my best friend, Eleanor, for quite some time in and around East Tawas, Michigan, much to the chagrin of ole Sheriff Peterson.

Eleanor cleared her throat, bringing me out of my thoughts. "I asked if you're okay, Agnes?"

I stared straight ahead on the road and turned into the drive of the notorious Butler Mansion. It's been the scene of more than one murder through the years, and Eleanor and I almost bought the big one ourselves in the mansion, but luckily, with our quick wits and a warning from the Butler descendants from beyond the grave, we managed to see the light of day. I didn't see a ghost that day, but we sure heard a warning just in time. We thoroughly believe that the ghosts of days gone by at the mansion didn't want us to die that day. Why, we'll never know.

I braked hard, and Eleanor and I, along with the ghostly apparition, left the confines of the car, striding toward the door. I rang the doorbell and waited for it to be answered, but after a few minutes, Eleanor slapped a hand against the door, impatiently knocking.

I stared curiously over at a blue Impala parked in the drive. "Someone has to be home."

The ghostly figure left the porch, walked toward the back yard and I followed suit. Perhaps it knew more than El or me.

"Let's check the back door," I called over to Eleanor who left the porch to follow me.

In the rear of the house, there were newly added French doors on the patio deck. The ghostly apparition didn't wait for us and glided through the door. Then, with a whoosh of air, the door magically opened a crack, enough for us to be able to push it open and enter the mansion.

"Maybe we shouldn't just go in," Eleanor said.

I whirled and gave her one of my looks, asking, "And why not?"

Eleanor fidgeted with a button on her shirt. "Well, every time we just up and waltz into a place we weren't let into, something dreadful happens, like the cops showing up."

I smiled. "Well, you're right about that, Eleanor, but we were expected," I said as I led the way inside.

Eleanor stopped right inside the door. "Maybe nobody is here yet to receive us."

"There's a car outside," I pointed out.

Eleanor shuddered as she gasped, "It's freezing in here. I just know this place is haunted."

I stared at the ghost, who seemed to be having a fit of the giggles, although soundless. "There's no such thing as ghosts." I said this so that Eleanor wouldn't run screaming from the mansion since we had promised to oversee preparations.

"Humph. What about that time in the attic when we heard a warning from a ghost?"

The ghost shrugged and I insisted, "There's no proof that it came from a ghost."

"No, b-but—"

"But nothing," I interjected. "Let's check out the place and see if someone might actually be here. There might be a legitimate reason why that door wasn't answered, and I fully intend to find out what it is."

With the ghost's arms folded across her chest, she nodded in agreement. I was quite positive by now that I had really lost it. Seeing a ghost can't be normal. I promised myself that I'd check with the doctor about the medication I was on, and soon.

The walnut walls smelled freshly cleaned with the fragrance of lemon oil that wafted in the air. As I neared the staircase, I saw the body of a woman crumpled at the foot of the stairs. I shook my head. We'd done it again—found yet another body. The strangest thing was it didn't nearly rattle me like it used to, since El and I routinely managed to find a body or two. But, I never looked forward to the questioning we'd be sure to get when the cops showed up.

Before I had a chance to spit out much of anything, Eleanor sputtered, "What did I tell you, Aggie? I told you we shouldn't have come inside. I told you it was a bad idea and now we're in a fix. We should call the sheriff from the car so we don't get into any trouble."

I narrowed my eyes. "What's the point? We already came inside, and it's from here we'll make our call."

Eleanor crossed her arms and sighed. "Oh, great. We'll be hauled off to jail for sure now."

"Eleanor, why would the sheriff do that when we've only just arrived?"

"Beats me, but you know how he feels about us getting involved in murder cases."

"Don't jump to any conclusions just yet. We don't even know how the woman might have died."

I dialed 911 and reported we'd found a body at the Butler Mansion, and then ended the call. I stepped closer to the body to get a better look. "Do you notice anything odd about her, Eleanor?"

"Not much besides that it's a body of a dead woman."

"How do you think she died?"

"Fell down the stairs."

I shook my head. "Wrong. Do you see any blood? Because I don't! If she had fallen down the stairs, she'd have wacked her head on the way down, or at least on the marble floor here."

"Sounds about right. Then how do you think she died?"

"Not sure, but it might not have happened here."

"So you think that—"

Eleanor never got a chance to finish what she was going to say when sirens sounded in close proximity, and flashers were visible through the sheer curtains of the drawing room from where they stood near the staircase.

I hurried over and let Trooper Sales inside. He was one of the Michigan State Police's finest, and married to my granddaughter, Sophia.

Sheriff Peterson entered next, yanking up his trousers, and instead of reading us the riot act, he simply asked, "Where's the body?"

Surprised but relieved, I led the way. "We just arrived. We were supposed to oversee the preparations of the mansion opening as a bed and breakfast," I explained.

"Sophia told me," Sales said. "Was the door open when you arrived?"

I froze as the ghost stood close by and pointed toward the French doors.

"Nobody came to the door when I knocked and when we came around back, the door somehow opened."

"Yes," Eleanor said. "Like a ghost opened it."

"Perhaps the latch is simply broken," I suggested, not willing to believe the ghost I kept seeing was real.

Sales checked for a pulse and asked, "And this is how you found the body?"

"Of course. I know better than to move it. I also couldn't help but notice that there's no blood, like you'd expect to see if she fell down the stairs."

"Oh, and what do you make of that?" Peterson asked.

"That her body was moved—that she might have been killed elsewhere."

"Good observation, but we don't know how she died just yet. We'll have to wait for the coroner's report," Peterson said.

"Her neck might be broken," Eleanor said. "But what are those marks on her neck? They look bite marks of some sort, like a vampire bit her or something."

I rushed over there to take a look, and sure enough, there were two puncture marks on her neck. "How odd, but I doubt that it's the work of a vampire, El, since they don't really exist."

"Says who? People told us Bigfoot wasn't real and look how that turned out."

"I'd rather forget, if you don't mind. Besides, Bigfoot hasn't been seen in quite some time."

"Do you know who this is, Agnes?" Peterson asked.

I rummaged through my purse, came back with a piece of paper, and read off the name, "Katherine Clark was the name of the woman we were supposed to meet here. I'm not certain it's her, but it most likely is."

"What do you know, if anything, about Katherine?" asked Peterson.

"Nothing at all. I was just told that she would be running the place. It looks like someone didn't want her to."

"And you've never had any contact with her before?"

"Nope."

Peterson turned in Eleanor's direction. "How about you, Eleanor?"

"I've spoken to her a few times on the phone. She had the nicest phone voice."

"When was the last time you spoke with her?"

Eleanor pressed a finger against her head. "Let me think. Yesterday afternoon. She wanted to make sure that Agnes and I showed up today to help her ready the mansion for their grand opening on Halloween."

"I see. Was that it?"

"Yup. That's about all of it."

"What do you mean *about* it?"

"Well, I was kinda excited. I drove past a few times and I couldn't help but notice a black sedan heading up the drive to the mansion."

Peterson took a step toward the body. "What do you make of that, Agnes?"

"I'll have to call Andrew and see if he can get ahold of the owner. I believe the actress, Sara Knoxville, owns the Butler Mansion. It might have been her at the mansion in the sedan."

I made my call and after I informed Andrew what we had found out at the mansion, he told us to stay put until he could get there.

I then informed Sales and Peterson that Andrew would be along presently, just as the meat wagon pulled up outside the mansion. One of the deputies let a portly man in the front door and he stumbled his way toward the body. The new medical examiner was an odd fellow who wore a Colombo-type raincoat that he always wore come rain or shine. Walter Smitty was his name.

Sales shook his head. "So we have a body that was positioned near the stairs that has suspicious markings on the neck."

"Very curious indeed," I said, ignoring the ghost who shook her head sadly.

Walter checked for Katherine's pulse and snapped the gum he chomped on. "Yup, she's dead alright, and boy am I hungry," he said as if we had a sandwich available to give to him.

"That sure ain't brain surgery," Eleanor said. "I could have said that for nothing."

"You could, but you're hardly qualified to, dear lady."

I positioned myself between Walter and Eleanor just in case she flew off the handle. "Yup. You're right. I sure hope you can get that autopsy done soon so we can figure out what happened here."

"The coroner will be doing it tomorrow, most likely. All I do is pronounce."

"Most medical examiners are public officials like the sheriff, and since he does a top notch job of investigating crimes in this county, I thought he could do that job," I said.

Peterson chuckled at that. "Thanks, but I could use all the help I can get since Halloween is right around the corner."

"Yup. It will soon be Halloween and we have a vampire on the loose," Eleanor said.

"In that case, you might want to start wearing garlic around your neck," Walter suggested. "Luckily, though, most of the vampires are only on television, not in a sleepy community such as Tawas, but what makes you think this is the work of a vampire anyway?"

I tried not to put too much significance to the 'vampire' part. "Well, there appear to be puncture marks on the victim's neck."

Walter took another look at the body. "Hardly the work of a vampire. It looks like fingernail marks to me."

"Perhaps we should search the mansion. You know, just in case the perp is hiding out here," I suggested to Peterson.

Trooper Sales sprinted up the stairs with an out-of-breath Sheriff Peterson behind him, while El and I cooled our heels downstairs. For the moment, my ghostly partner in crime seemed to be absent; that is, if she was even there at all. Instead of feeling relieved, I sort of missed having her around, even though I knew how nuts that sounded.

So lost in thought was I, that I jumped at the sound of a knock at the door. The ghostly figure appeared out of the ceiling, waiting patiently as I opened the door to Andrew, giving him a quick hug as he came in.

"What happened?" Andrew asked.

"Well—"

Before I was able to really give him the rundown, Walter Smitty piped up and said, "They found the yet-unidentified body of a woman at the bottom of the steps and called us in to deal with it." He paused for a moment before continuing. "I don't know why Sheriff Peterson doesn't just appoint these two as honorary deputies. From the word around town, they won't butt out of the sheriff's cases."

"Please don't encourage them," Andrew said as he massaged the back of his neck. "I've been trying to tell Agnes to mind her own business for quite a while now, but even I have to admit that she and Eleanor are quite good at putting clues together."

"That's always a good thing, but I need to get this corpse back to the morgue so the coroner can do an autopsy to determine the cause of death."

"You must have some kind of idea how the victim died," Andrew said, with the ghost nodding behind him.

"Not sure just yet, but her neck might be broken. There's no sign of blunt force trauma."

I was intent on staring at the ghost until Eleanor asked, "Why on earth are you looking at the wall like that, Aggie? Blood splatter?"

I whirled around really quick, or as quick as a woman of seventy-two can whirl. "Nope. Ever since my accident I haven't been quite right."

"I'd say way before that, but I understand, dear." El puffed up her chest. "I really thought I had lost you that time."

"I'm sorry. I've been in such a weird mood of late and I really need to make a doctor's appointment soon. My head feels so foggy lately."

"It's to be expected, Aggie," Andrew said. "I had another case in Detroit, but I'm having an associate handle it. I'm just not ready to leave you so soon since the accident. Plus, I don't think your son likes me all that much. It might be a good idea to get to know Stuart."

"That makes two of us. If truth be known ... I don't know my son all that well these days, either."

"When was the last time you saw him?"

"Not since he graduated from college, but that was ten years ago. It seems that both of my children have all sorts of reasons to stay away."

"That's not true," Eleanor said. "Martha is a free spirit and went on a 'finding herself road trip', but she eventually came to town looking for you."

"Yup. When she was out of money, that is."

"You, too?" Walter asked. "Children have a way of doing that, but with the economy like it is, I can't say I blame them. It's not like you can find high paying jobs these days. All of the factories have closed or sold out. I remember a time when US 23 had many businesses, but now, most of them have closed down."

"Walter, I had no idea that you have lived in Tawas that long," El said.

"I haven't, but it's been a great vacation spot for my wife and the family."

Sheriff Peterson and Trooper Sales came back down the stairs, and Peterson announced, "The upper floors are clear. We'll be checking the first floor and cellar."

"Cellar?" I asked. "I had no idea there was a cellar here."

"Oh, and how well do you think you know the Butler Mansion? Have you inspected every square inch during earlier cases?"

I clammed up when the ghost shook her head. "Nope. Knock yourself out. Can we leave now? I don't expect that you'll allow us to inspect the mansion ourselves, so we'll do it at a later date."

"We plan to put up police tape. It's a crime scene."

"Yup, sure is. Too many to count, but don't forget that the actress, Sara Knoxville owns this place and is opening a bed and breakfast soon and we were hired to oversee things."

Peterson laughed. "Well, in that case it seems like you're off to a good start."

I chose to ignore that barb sent my way. We moved to leave and I snickered as the ghost made a motion like it was giving Peterson a swift kick in the pants. Once we were outside, Andrew convinced us to ride with him since I had already admitted that my head was a bit fuzzy. Instead of arguing with him as I had a wont to do, I let it drop since it made all the sense in the world.

Once we were settled in Andrew's SUV, with Eleanor in the front seat as it allowed for more room for her, and the ghost sitting next to me, off we went. On the journey to Eleanor's place, I called Doctor Thomas, who agreed to meet me in an hour. He was the sort of doctor who made house calls, but since he lived a few doors down from Eleanor's cottage on Lake Huron, it was hardly an imposition.

CHAPTER TWO

Eleanor led the way inside her house, inviting Dr. Thomas, who was already waiting in the driveway in his red sports car, inside. I tried to get a good look at the occupant in the passenger seat, but it was really none of my concern. Word is that the good doctor prefers the company of men, but nobody even gives it a second thought since he's a staple in the community, and the only doctor who makes house calls.

Eleanor busied herself in the kitchen, rustling up ice tea, while Dr. Thomas joined me outside on the deck. Andrew was kind enough to allow us privacy when I told him I wanted to speak to the good doctor alone. Thankfully, the ghost also took her leave.

I sat on a wicker chair and motioned Dr. Thomas to a chair next to me.

Dr. Thomas raised a brow on his handsome face. "What's the problem, Agnes?"

I fidgeted. How does one ask a doctor a question like the one I needed to ask? "Well," I began. "I was just wondering about the medication I'm on."

"Are you having some kind of reaction?"

"W-Would it cause me to see things, like things that aren't there?"

Dr. Thomas pulled out his iPhone and began to punch at the buttons on the screen. "You're not on anything too heavy duty. Vicodin can cause drowsiness, anxiety, and nervousness. You're not taking Tylenol with it, are you?"

"No. So it can't cause me seeing things then?"

"No, but just to be safe it might be better to quit taking it if you're concerned. Perhaps it might be a good idea to come back to the hospital and get a CT scan."

"A CT scan? I'll quit taking the pain meds. I'll just take Tylenol if I get any more headaches."

"You're still getting headaches?"

"Yes, but they're not all that bad. I'd really hate to have a CT scan, but it might be a good idea just to make sure everything looks okay."

"You sure took quite a blow to your head in the accident. Perhaps it might be best to take time away from your investigative duties. At least until you are feeling better."

I massaged my brow and stood as Dr. Thomas handed me a slip of paper with the written orders for the CT scan. This sure was the last thing I wanted to do, but I wanted to be sure that I could rule out any medical condition that might be causing me to see the ghost.

Andrew took me to the hospital and I had the test, but while I was readying to go back home, I noticed the ghost was still strangely missing. The funny thing was, I kinda missed her. I mean I had gotten used to seeing the apparition.

Once Andrew pulled into my drive, it was beginning to get dark. I really had to admit that I was quite tired. Andrew sacked out on the couch and Duchess, my cat, leapt on his lap, enjoying the petting she got and purring loudly to the amusement of Andrew. Duchess had hissed at Andrew when we first began dating, but now she sure enjoyed the special attention he gave her. I, on the other hand, had felt too under the weather of late. It wasn't like I had been ignoring my cat on purpose. She glanced over at me lazily, like she knew I was thinking about her.

I wandered down the hallway and dressed in my pajamas, crawling into bed. I smiled to myself since the ghost was missing. Perhaps I might just wake up refreshed in the morning and find out this was all a bad dream, or that's what I kept telling myself. It's been hard keeping a secret this big from everyone I love, but the truth was that I worried they might just lock me away in an institution.

It wasn't long before I nodded off, catching the fragrance of vanilla, which was too hard to ignore, but at that point, I wasn't willing to think it meant anything. All I know is that I have smelled vanilla from time to time without any real reason. I didn't currently have any flowers, even in the house, and I was all out of my room freshener that shoots fragrance in the air every half hour or so.

I yawned once I got out of bed in the morning and headed straight for the shower. I'm quite the creature of habit. If I don't take a shower straight away, I won't take one until well into the afternoon, but since Eleanor and I have some investigating to do, I hardly had time to laze around.

By the time I finished my shower and was dressed comfortably in blue crop pants and white shirt with an anchor over the lone pocket, I strode into the kitchen where my handsome fiancé, Andrew, awaited me with a cup of freshly brewed coffee. And this time when I smelled vanilla, I knew it was from the vanilla creamer I always use. A little coffee with my cream, Andrew always said.

"It sure was cold in here last night," Andrew remarked. "I froze all night. Even checked to see if the air-conditioner was on."

I froze for a moment, but said, "Well, it is October. We get quite cool nights now, especially since we're so near to Lake Huron."

"Oh, I know, but I could have sworn…" He paused. "Oh, never mind. You'd think that I'm crazy."

I lifted my coffee mug that Andrew had poured for me with the creamer already added. "What? Do tell?"

"It's just that every time I'm near you, I can't help but wonder if we're really alone—even when we are. Perhaps it was being back at the Butler Mansion again. I'm not sure why Sara Knoxville even wants to open up a bed and breakfast there. Not with all the murders that have happened on the property."

I sipped my coffee and smiled appreciatively. "I'm sure it seems interesting to her. Look at how popular paranormal reality television is of late. She could play off the paranormal activity part even."

"She's hardly that type of woman."

"Oh, I know, but I wouldn't be surprised if some of her Hollywood friends showed up in town to check out the place."

Andrew washed his coffee cup and carefully put it on the drain board. "I don't take her for a manipulative woman, or someone who believes in ghosts."

"I never said she was, just that with Halloween coming—"

"That it might be a good time to exploit the haunted history of the place."

"We can't say it's haunted at all, since I've never seen any ghosts there," I lied. But in truth, I can't say the ghost I had seen had anything to do with the ghosts that might be at the mansion.

"I guess you can believe anything you want to, but there's something about that mansion that bugs me."

"Well, another body showed up, but Eleanor and I will be investigating the death of Katherine Clark for sure.

"I expected as much, but you really should be resting more. I'm not ready to spend any more nights at the hospital at your bedside."

"Well, don't then."

"What? And face the wrath of your son, Stuart? I can tell already that he doesn't care for me."

"I can't blame him." When Andrew gave me a cockeyed look, I continued. "I mean, neither of us knows all that much about Stuart just yet. I'm about as nervous around him as you. I haven't had time to sit down and have a heart-to-heart with him, but I really should do that today. I'd hate to get too wrapped up in a murder investigation when I have personal matters to attend to."

"Good thinking, Agnes, because he'll be here shortly. "When I called him last night about your CT scan, he insisted he visit you, and soon."

I eyed Andrew's white pants and button-up Hawaiian-style shirt that he wore the day before. "Which is why it might be best if you change."

"What would you like me to change into, Aggie? One of those shifters that have taken over the book market of late?"

"You could do worse than being a werewolf or werebear, I suppose."

"Yes, like a vampire, but the medical examiner shot that theory down."

I pulled out my pink ruffled bathrobe for Andrew, who then threw his clothes in the washer. Right then there was a hard knock on the door. I opened the door to Stuart's tanned and handsome face. He looked so like his father, who had died at age forty of a heart attack.

Stuart walked inside and raised a brow sharply at Andrew's ensemble. "What are you doing here?" Stuart wanted to know, not a bit of a smile on his face.

Andrew lounged on the couch and said, "Your mother thought I should wash my clothing so I don't look out of place in town later."

"With a town as small as East Tawas, I'm sure everyone knows what you wore yesterday."

"Stuart," I butted in. "Andrew is my fiancé."

"Why on earth would you want to get married at your age, Mother?"

I frowned. "I don't like the sound of that. Plenty of women my age get married."

"Really? Like who, specifically?"

I puffed up my chest. "Well, Eleanor has a fiancé, too. She is engaged to Mr. Wilson. Are you planning to chastise her, too, or call her old?"

Stuart gave me a blank expression. "Not at all, Mother, but you're not getting any younger. You can't just hook up with anyone these days, you know."

I would have smiled at Stuart's protectiveness if it weren't for Andrew, who cocked a brow. "Hook up with? Is that any way to speak to your mother, who, for the record, you haven't seen in, like, ten years?"

"I just don't want you taken for a fool is all, and Andrew sure looks foolish in that robe of yours."

Andrew laughed outright. "I'll agree with you there, Stuart, but I assure you that I'm not setting out to hurt your mother in any kind of way. I love her, for one, and she's sharp as a tack. I can't see getting anything past her."

"Andrew's an attorney," I added. "I worked for him years ago in Saginaw. We reconnected when he came to East Tawas."

"What Aggie means is that she was only employed by me back in Saginaw. I was very married then and there was no funny business going on."

Stuart took the cup of coffee I offered and asked, "So why did you suddenly show up in East Tawas?"

I gasped. "Really, Stuart! Why are you interrogating Andrew like this?"

"Because I want to know the particulars before I give my blessing."

Andrew stood up and stretched, making way for the kitchen that was open to the living room with only a round kitchen table separating it. He poured a cup of coffee and rubbed his hands briskly. I didn't have to know why, as the ghostly figure floated from the ceiling and now hovered near Stuart with a huge smile on her face.

Andrew leaned against the kitchen counter and answered Stuart's question.
"I came to town with a friend. His daughter disappeared in Tadium and Agnes was kind enough to offer her help."

"That's another thing. What is this I hear about you investigating crimes, Mother?"

I plopped down on the sofa. This was going to be a long conversation. "Not much to say about it, really, just that Eleanor and I have a knack for solving mysteries and I'm not going to sit here and have an in-depth conversation about it."

"Which means what?"

"Save your breath, Stuart," Andrew began. "I don't approve either, but there's no telling her to stop doing whatever she sets her mind to do. I've tried and failed on many occasions."

"You do know that's what the cops are for, right? That you are only complicating cases with your meddling."

"That's not true. Eleanor and I come up with some pretty solid leads at times and have solved numerous cases. Even Sheriff Peterson doesn't get all that mad anymore, and we always keep him abreast of what we find out once we figure out it's a solid lead."

"Martha told me all about it. She also mentioned that you and Eleanor barely escaped with your lives several times."

"Yes, but the cops always show up to save the day and arrest the bad guys or gals."

"I see. Well, you're both too old to get yourselves into danger. It's dangerous enough with all the accidents old folks can have right at home. Now that I'm in town, things are going to change."

My heart about leapt out of my body at his last statement and the ghost just shook her head. "You can say all you want, but don't think for a minute that I plan to change my ways with you here in town. If you're so concerned about me, why have you stayed out of my life so long?"

Stuart sat on a chair opposite me. "I went to college and graduated with a bachelor's degree in history. After college, I traveled extensively, and Martha called me after your accident."

Traveled extensively? "How were you able to travel so extensively? What do you do for a living?"

"I took part in a research project after college and I spent most of my time abroad studying ancient civilizations."

"No wonder I haven't heard from you. You could have at least invited me to your college graduation."

"I'm sorry about that, but I'm here now. I really would like to see you and Eleanor cool it on your investigative activities."

At least he was toning down his attitude. "I can't do that. Yesterday, we found a body at the Butler Mansion." I then updated Stuart on what happened, excluding the part about the ghost I've been seeing, who was currently stroking Stuart's face without him knowing it, since he didn't even react.

This ghost is sure turning out to be quite mischievous. Now I had two mysteries on my hands, or three if you count Stuart's half-baked story about traveling abroad to study ancient civilizations. Who really killed the woman at the mansion, who was this ghost really; and just why has she attached herself to me? It was bad enough that I wasn't ready to tell Eleanor or anyone else about my ghostly encounters. I had no idea how I'd be able to keep it all a secret.

Stuart interrupted my thoughts when he asked, "So how do you plan to find out who murdered the woman at the mansion?"

Before I was able to open my mouth, Stuart's cell rang and he answered it, but didn't say a word. He then powered off the phone with a flick of his finger and said, "Hold that thought for another time. I'll see you later, Mother." He hiked out the door and I watched from the window as he hopped on a black crotch rocket, a Kawasaki Ninja motorcycle, and tore off down the drive.

"Well, he sure lit out of here fast," I said.

"Probably for the best, since his advice won't be followed by you."

I ignored the ghost, who currently pouting by the door. "Good on both accounts. I'm sorry he treated you like that. I just can't imagine why he thinks you're one of the bad guys."

"It's perfectly understandable. He's just being protective. If I were him, I'd be the same way."

I supposed, but it still bothered me that Stuart insinuated that Andrew was no good when he hadn't even seen me in ten years. Hopefully in time, that would change.

CHAPTER THREE

An hour later, Andrew was dressed in his clean clothes and made an excuse that he had business to attend to in regards to picking up Sara Knoxville from the airport, but he did take me back to the Butler Mansion to retrieve my car.

After Andrew roared off down the road, I stared at the yellow police tape that was strewn across the front door. Drat it. I really wanted to go inside for a quick peek, but Eleanor wasn't with me and that wouldn't be right, so I drove to her house and picked her up.

Once Eleanor was seated in the passenger's seat, I admired her yellow pantsuit with white tank top beneath its jacket. "You sure look great today, but won't you get hot?"

"Not lately. It's October, don't you know?"

"Yes, but it's in the seventies, dear."

"Are we going to discuss suitable apparel all day or check out the Butler Mansion? You did say that Andrew was picking up the owner, Sara Knoxville, right?"

"Yes, of course."

I cranked over the engine and off we went with my ghostly passenger in the back, who toppled over as I shot off. I snickered for a moment until Eleanor gave me a hard stare. "What's so funny?" she wanted to know.

"Oh, nothing, really. It's just funny that we're going back to poke around in the mansion again. I hope we're able to search it before Andrew brings Sara there."

"I can't imagine an actress staying at the mansion."

"Why not, El? It has much better accommodations than most of the hotels around East Tawas."

"Not so sure about that. If she stays at the East Tawas Beach Resort, she can order room service."

"You're right there. I guess we'll find out soon enough."

"Hey, Aggie. I sure hope she brings some famous actors or actresses with her, like Brad Pitt and Angelina Jolie."

I about spit out my uppers. "Seriously? I doubt you'd see anyone that big showing up in town, but she might bring someone with her. I'm not even sure if she's married."

"Not according to the tabloids," Eleanor said. "They barely mention her unless she attends a movie premiere."

"Lucky for her. I can't imagine anyone famous would want to be in a tabloid at all since most of the stories are complete fabrications of the truth."

"That's not true. I've seen impending divorces turn into real ones even though both parties have denied it."

"Hmmm. What is Sara Knoxville famous for, exactly?"

Eleanor gripped her big black bag. "Oh, you know, she was in that thing about the beach and another about a wedding."

"Oh, and those are the names of movies?"

"You know my mind isn't always the swiftest."

"Neither is mine most of the time, but there are so many movies about weddings that I can hardly keep track. I suppose I could ask Sara when I see her."

I pulled into the mansion's drive and it was empty except for the Impala. When Eleanor and I stepped out of the car, I made tracks to the Impala, trying the doors, but they were all locked. "Oh, phooey," I said.

"You actually expected to find the doors open? That would be too easy. If it is Katherine's car, I'm surprised it wasn't hauled off to impound."

"Perhaps because it's not hers."

The ghost floated toward the backyard like she had before, but the door was already ajar by the time we caught up. "Did you do that?" I asked the ghost.

"Did I do what?" Eleanor asked. "I didn't do anything."

With an exhale of breath, I walked inside with Eleanor nearly hugging me, she was so close. "Oh, nothing, I was just thinking out loud."

"You better cut that out. It's becoming a habit with you lately."

I shook Eleanor off me. "You don't need to stand that close to me, El. I can barely breathe as it is."

"Not sure why. It can't have anything to do with the fact that we can see our breath inside," she said as she puffed out a breath, and sure enough, the white mist appeared from between her lips like it does during winter.

"That's sure strange. It is a tad cold in here, I suppose. Perhaps the air conditioning is on." I went to check the thermostat, but it was off.

"Since when can you see your breath with the air conditioning on? No system ever makes it that cold," Eleanor said with chattering teeth. "I-I think this place is haunted for real."

I wasn't about to admit to that. The ghost hovered close by, her eyes focused behind us and in the direction of the stairs. I slowly turned, and saw a mist making its way up the stairs.

Eleanor followed my line of vision and asked, "I-Is th-that a-a gh-ghost?"

I made way for the stairs. "We should check out the upstairs."

Eleanor threw her arms wide. "Are you nuts? I'm not searching a real haunted mansion. I'd rather deal with finding a dead body than a ghost. Corpses can't hurt you."

My hands went to my hips. "And neither can ghosts, if that even was one. We might just find out that a ray of light has filtered from somewhere upstairs."

"Well, I'm not going up there."

"Fine, then I'll go by myself." I flicked the lights on but nothing happened. "That's odd. The power must not be on yet."

"That's what the ghosts want you to believe. They're gonna lure us up there and push us back down the stairs or something. No way am I going up there."

"Fine, then stay down here all by yourself."

"To hell with being in here at all. I'm leaving."

Eleanor ran for the door that was pushed shut by my ghostly escort, and she must have locked it, too, since Eleanor rattled the door something fierce. "I want out of here."

"Eleanor Mason. Come here now and quit being such a big baby. There are no such things as ghosts."

"Then how did the door slam shut, and how is it now locked?"

"Cross breeze, probably. You know old mansions like this have plenty of drafts. Since you can't go out, you might as well join me upstairs, unless you want to wait for a ghost to get you down here."

The ghost laughed and gave Eleanor a nudge. Eleanor whirled, racing to my side. "I felt something touch me," El said with tears swimming in her eyes.

"Not to worry. Even if this place is haunted, I won't let them hurt you. I promise."

"Your promises might not be so good if we both meet our end here, but I'll go upstairs to check it out since you refuse to leave."

I grabbed the banister and climbed the stairs slowly so as not to lose my footing since it was darker on the stairs than it was downstairs. When I reached the second floor, I yanked my cell phone out, but right before I was able to power on the flashlight tool, the lights flickered on. I froze for a moment until my ghostly companion joined us. The ghost was starting to make me feel at ease with her presence. She sure was less scary than seeing another ghost.

"Hey, Eleanor. So you saw the ghost go up the stairs?"

"Yes. You did too, right?"

"Yes, but is that the only ghost you saw?"

Eleanor gripped my arm in a death-like grip. "You mean there's more?"

"I'm not sure just yet, I was just checking. This mansion could be filled with them from the amount of murders that have happened here, and those are the only ones we know about." I turned to the right and headed down the corridor. "Let's see. There was Herman Butler and the handyman."

"Don't forget Mildred Winfree," Eleanor added. "The thing is, there might be more that we never heard about in the past. We should do some research on the mansion. It's a mighty unlucky place."

"Exactly." I tried not looking at the portraits of the Butler descendants that hung side by side on the walls of the corridor. Why, the eyes seemed to almost follow us as we walked. I shook my head. *Stop it, Agnes, you're losing it.*

I stopped at the end of the hall and went into the first room, ignoring the squeak of the door when it opened. I scanned the boxes stacked in the room. "Looks like just a storage room," I said. I made my way back into the hallway and we searched the next room that was a bedroom. Each room had the same ornate, Elizabethan antique four-poster bed with tapestry. The colors ranged from green to deep burgundy, colors that were used during the same period. "Sara Knoxville certainly has gone all out turning this into a bed and breakfast that will awe the visitors."

"I wonder. I guess we'll have to ask her when she gets here. I can't imagine that she was able to furnish the place so elaborately. It would cost quite a bit to stay at this place and most folks in East Tawas don't have that kind of money."

"Tourists might. I wonder if she plans to tell anyone about the dark history of the place. It might keep the place packed."

"What?" Eleanor choked out. "Who'd want to sleep in a murder mansion?"

"Not us, but there are many people who are into that sort of thing. If they advertised the place was haunted it would even pack up more."

"I don't know this Sara Knoxville yet, but I can't image anyone trying to take advantage of that kind of history. Besides, it's not a proven fact that the mansion is haunted at all."

At least Eleanor was on the same page with me. "Exactly. Let's check that last door and we can leave, since I don't see anything of much interest here."

When we went into the last room at the opposite side of the corridor, there were containers of makeup on the dresser, and the closet door was opened a crack. I went over there and checked out the inside of the closet. At first, I thought it was empty, but as I ran my fingers along the back, I felt the ridge of a handle of a suitcase. I removed it and put it on the bed. "Looks like the sheriff missed something."

I tried to open the suitcase, but it was locked. I pounded on it in frustration, and the ghost put her hand through it and then it snapped open. Eleanor backed up a tad. "How did you do that?"

"Beats me, but at least we can check it out now."

I moved the contents to the side that were mostly clothing, but underneath were envelopes addressed to Katherine Clark, so I figured we were onto something.

I handed Eleanor the envelopes and she said, "Should we really be going through Katherine's personal effects? It feels kinda intrusive."

"Probably not, but we really need to find a clue or two if we're going to figure out who might have murdered Katherine." I took the mail from Eleanor and went to put in back in the suitcase. "Perhaps you're right. We should take the suitcase to the sheriff's department."

"No need to get hasty, Agnes. I just meant it seems wrong, not that I wasn't willing to take a look-see. Then you can take it to the sheriff."

I handed the mail back to Eleanor, who carefully tucked it inside her purse. "Anything of interest besides the mail?"

"Nope."

Eleanor came over and fingered the fabric on the inside of the suitcase. "No hidden compartments."

"Why would you think there'd be a hidden compartment in a suitcase?"

"Good point. We should check out the inside of the closet instead."

Before I could say anything, Eleanor was face first in the closet, slapping her palms on the walls, her round bottom nearly in my face.

"Eleanor, please. You're not going to find anything in there." I stared at the bookshelf next to the closet and began to pull books out. Suddenly, the entire closet rolled to the side. Poor Eleanor barely had time to move out of the way before it disappeared into the wall. We both stared, wide-eyed, at a door behind the closet and before I gave it much thought, I opened it. On the other side was an opening that led to a hidden passageway.

I stared at the cobwebs with little enthusiasm. "This sure looks interesting, but being surrounded by spiders—not so much."

"Since when are you afraid of a little adventure? And those are probably only cobwebs."

"Oh? So you're not worried about meeting up with a gigantic spider?"

"Nope. Because you're going to check it out—not me."

I reared back. "What? Why me? My name isn't Indiana Jones."

"Because you're younger, dear."

"Yes, but old enough to know better than to be walking down some corridor where I might break something. Who knows the condition of the inside, or what else might be in there?"

"I suppose, but it's worth the challenge, isn't it? You might discover treasure down there."

"Or meet my maker, which I'm so not ready to do just yet."

I looked for the ghost for emotional support, but she was already headed through the opening. I had to follow, but I really hated to be covered with cobwebs so I yanked a sheet off the bed and threw it over my head, gathering it beneath my chin.

"Good thinking, Aggie," Eleanor said.

With the light from my iPhone, I led the way inside. The floor beneath our feet was wood, and clumps of hair were gathered in the corners. "This looks like animal hair," I observed.

"I sure hope not from rats," Eleanor said.

At some point, I lost sight of the ghost and then I felt a breeze blow on me from above. I stared upward, but I figured it must have come from the ductwork so I continued. Before we knew it, there was a set of stairs to descend, which made sense since we were on the second floor.

I jumped when the ghost glided toward me with a smile on her face. She then turned around and led us deeper down the hallway. There was a light at the end of the tunnel, and once we neared it, I shoved hanging vines aside and stepped out into the sunshine. I gasped when I saw we were standing in the Butler's family cemetery. "Well, I'll be. I sure never expected the pathway to lead to the cemetery."

"Me, either," Eleanor said. "But it must have been there for a reason. I just don't understand why anyone would want to leave the comforts of the mansion to be out here in the graveyard?"

"Someone with something to hide, like their comings and goings."

"Well, whoever that was had to have been one the original owners because that pathway had to have been put in long ago."

"Exactly. It also means that anyone could come into the mansion undetected and leave without anyone knowing."

"Aggie, do you think that whoever killed Katherine might have used this passageway to escape after they murdered her?"

"Not sure, but it makes perfect sense. I can't help but wonder who knows that much about the mansion to perpetrate the crime."

"So, not only do we need to find out more about who Katherine really is, but the history about the mansion, and hopefully we'll find out who might have wanted the poor girl dead."

"At this point, we don't know all that much about her other than she was readying the mansion for the bed and breakfast opening," I mused.

"With Sara Knoxville coming to town, we might get some answers."

"Not so sure about that, though. She's only inherited the mansion since her father met his demise, but I suppose there's no reason to think negative just yet."

Eleanor and I made our way back into the mansion and brushed our clothes off the best we could, concealing the opening again. Also the sheet I had worn was tossed in a nearby chair. The ghost floated alongside us as we made our way down the stairs.

When I stepped back on the first floor, Andrew stared me down. There was a beautiful blonde standing next to him with a puzzled look on her face. "Hello, there," I greeted them.

Andrew knocked the dust from my shoulder. "What on earth have you two been up to? You both look like you've been cleaning the chimney."

"We've been looking for clues."

"Where? Under the beds? Or in the cellar?"

"We thought we saw something strange."

"Like what?"

"Not really sure, but Eleanor seems to think this place is haunted, if you can believe that."

"You thought that, too, Aggie."

"I'm really not positive what I saw, but if it was a ghost, it sure disappeared when we followed it upstairs."

Sara grinned, fanning her delicate face with her hand. "That sounds cool! I wish I could see a ghost firsthand."

"Be careful what you wish for," I said, nodding to the ghost hovering close by.

Andrew's brow shot up. "Whatever are you looking at, Agnes?"

"Nothing, but it looks like this place could still use a little dusting."

"I'll hire a cleaning crew right away," Sara said as she was about to make a call.

"Actually, we better get the go-ahead from Sheriff Peterson before we go into a cleaning phase. I'm not at all sure if they're done with this crime scene yet."

"Oh," Andrew said. "Then why are you two here?"

"We wanted to check for clues about Katherine's untimely death."

Sara bit her fist. "Oh, that's so awful. I still can't believe so many people have died on the grounds."

"Do tell."

Before Sara could respond, Eleanor asked, "Like recently or in the past?"

"Both, but perhaps we could discuss that at a later date, because the sheriff over there doesn't look too pleased that we're here."

Sure enough, Sheriff Peterson's frame filled the doorway, his nostril's flaring like a bull about to charge. "Why are you all here? Didn't you see the police tape?"

Sara sauntered over on her sky-high heels. Her ruby red lips parted and she smiled up at him. "Oh, I'm sorry, sheriff. I just flew into town and had to come here straightaway. It's just dreadful what happened to Katherine." She pulled off her sweater, revealing a white camisole top beneath that displayed her cleavage nicely. "But you must understand, I have to have this place ready for the grand opening on Halloween."

32

Peterson eyes drifted to Sara's cleavage and then he looked away as if they burned. His eyes looked anywhere except at Sara. "I see. W-Well, let me call the state police to assure they are finished here."

He strode outside to his squad car and Eleanor said, "Wow, I don't think I've ever seen Peterson do an about-face like that before."

"Boobs do have their uses," Sara said with a giggle.

Peterson came back in and gave us the all clear. "Agnes, can I speak with you outside?"

Eleanor and I followed him to his car where he leaned up against it. "I'm certainly no fool. You know better than to cross police tape."

I tried not to burst out in laughter as the ghost stuck her tongue out at Peterson. "Oh, I know," I finally said.

"Except that we came in the back door where there wasn't any police tape," Eleanor added, her eyes dancing in amusement. "And Sara and Andrew just showed up."

Peterson sighed. "Whatever. We've been at this for a while now, Agnes. Did you find any clues that we missed?"

"Actually, yes."

Eleanor's eyes widened to the degree that I thought they might pop out of her head.

"I found a suitcase, but it was only filled with clothing. It was in the back of a closet."

We were marched back inside and led the way up the stairs and into the room where we had found the suitcase ... but it was gone!

"I swear it was right here," I said in a panic.

Eleanor was about as shocked as I was and raced to the closet, searching for it there, but came up empty. She simply shrugged. "There is something strange going on in this mansion."

"Oh, besides the two of you?"

"No, I swear it was here. Why would I tell you we found something if we hadn't?"

"Is it possible Andrew or Sara took it?"

I gulped. "They just got here and we never even told them about finding anything."

Peterson picked off a web from my shoulder. "Why do the both of you look so dusty?"

"We were cleaning," we chimed together, as if on cue.

"Where? The attic?"

"No, we never even went up there."

"Nope," Eleanor added. "We're not about to go up there. It's haunted for sure."

"Haunted? Are you back to that nonsense? I sure hope you're not planning to call in those guys from G.A.S.P. again."

Ghost Association Special Police, or G.A.S.P., had caused quite the stir in town before, and at this very same mansion in the past. They even recorded a ghostly voice in that third floor room.

"I never said that, and from the sounds of it, Sara doesn't need any more delays. Halloween is in a few days. It sure doesn't give us much time to ready the place."

"What do you mean? Like the both of you will be helping out here?"

"Yes, we agreed to ready the mansion for the grand opening. Andrew is Sara's attorney."

Peterson swept a hand over his hair that was quite wet from sweat, like always. "I don't like the idea of either of you being here. It's dangerous. We don't know yet if Katherine was murdered."

"So you're not sure at this point if she died of natural causes?"

"We'll be continuing our investigation into Katherine's death unless the coroner's report states that she died of natural causes. As of now her death has been ruled as suspicious." Peterson glanced around as if to make sure we weren't overheard. "We currently have no leads in the case."

"Well, I know Katherine is new in town—possibly too new to have formed all that many connections."

"Exactly. I'll take my leave now, but if you ever find that suitcase, bring it down to the sheriff's department." He turned to leave, but turned back one last time and said, "Be careful, ladies. I don't think the East Tawas area would be able to handle it if anything happened to the two of you. You're local celebrities around here." With that, he left.

Eleanor grabbed my arms and turned me to face her. "Agnes, what do you think happened to that suitcase?"

"I have no idea, but it sure is bothersome. Do you remember seeing it when we came back in from the corridor?"

"Shucks, I can't remember."

"If it wasn't, it would mean that someone might have been inside the mansion when we were or hidden in the secret passageway. We might have been in danger the whole time."

"Well, Agnes, the door was ajar when we got here."

That bothered me, too. At the time, I thought the ghost had opened the door for us like the last time, but now I wasn't sure and wouldn't be able to ask the ghost with Eleanor present, but just then the ghost shook her head sadly and I knew she wasn't responsible for opening the door.

CHAPTER FOUR

What's going on here, ladies?" Sara asked as she waltzed into the room.

Eleanor's arms dropped from mine. "Well, Sheriff Peterson wanted to first assure himself that none of Katherine's personal effects remain in the mansion."

Her lips formed a big O. "I hope you ladies aren't too weirded-out now. I really could use your help. The cleaning crew will be here in a few hours and I was hoping you could supervise." When I gave her a puzzled look, she added, "Gather your belongings, girls. It would be great if you could stay here to oversee preparations."

Under any other circumstances, the chance to stay at the mansion would sound great, but now I really was concerned about our safety. "I'd feel better if the mansion was searched. I hate the thought that the murderer might be lurking somewhere."

Andrew volunteered to search the mansion for us when we met him downstairs, and while he was doing just that, I gave Sara a suggestion. "It might be wise to have the locks changed."

Her shoulders slumped. "Again? I've done that a few times already."

"You have?"

"Yes. I just don't see how anyone can get into the mansion unless they are let inside by someone."

"Okay, whatever you feel is best. Eleanor and I will have to go and gather our belongings. Is it okay if I bring my cat, Duchess? I just can't leave her all alone in the house. Poor dear has been sick of late."

"Sure, but be back here in an hour. I want someone to be here to let in the cleaners." She handed us the keys and told us that she'd be staying at the Tawas Beach Resort.

"So you won't be staying here, too?" I asked.

"I'm an actress, and it's unheard of me to stay somewhere while preparations are being made for an opening. I need to make my grand entrance," Sara said with a wink. "I have complete faith that you ladies can handle the details."

I drove to Eleanor's house in relative silence. It bothered me now that we were expected to stay at the mansion, and Eleanor mirrored my thoughts when she said, "I just don't like the idea of staying at the Butler Mansion now. It just doesn't feel safe."

"I agree, but we already made a commitment, one we can't just back out of."

Eleanor groaned. "I know, but we need to find some way to cover the opening that leads from the cemetery. It might be how the murderer accessed the mansion."

"Yes, but that wouldn't explain why the back door was open when we got there."

I skidded to a stop in Eleanor's driveway, and after the dust settled, we made way for the front door. Eleanor stared at the dirty dishes in the sink and I went to work on washing them while Eleanor gathered her belongings.

After I was done and had sat on the deck, admiring the view of Lake Huron for a time, Eleanor came panting into the room. "Whewie, my suitcase is sure heavy."

The waves lapped the shore as a speedboat whizzed by and I breathed in the fragrance of the lake that you can get nowhere other than Lake Huron. Sea gulls swooped low, scooped up fish and flew off with a hum of flapping wings.

I really didn't want to move from the lawn chair, but I finally did with a groan. When I went into Eleanor's room, her suitcase was so packed that there was no way that it would ever close.

"Eleanor, did you pack all of your belongings in the suitcase?"

"No, but I wanted to come prepared."

"How about just taking three outfits and leave the rest behind? I'm sure there's a washer and dryer at the mansion."

We spent the next ten minutes sorting through the items, deciding on a pink, purple, and green outfit. Next, the toiletries were added and makeup that included a godawful shade of red lipstick. The suitcase now closed easily, but it still was quite weighty as we lugged it to the car and put it in the trunk.

Soon, we were off down the road toward my house and I glanced at the clock and groaned inwardly. "We'll never be there in time for when the cleaning crew shows up."

"Maybe they'll be late," Eleanor said.

"Hopefully." When we arrived at my house ten short minutes later, items flew into my suitcase, and I lugged the suitcase out to the car and, of course, the cat supplies. I then spent a half-hour chasing Duchess around the house. I think she thought it was a game, but I was less than amused. It was then that I saw the ghost and wondered if her presence might be the problem. "Would you mind?" I said.

The ghost disappeared in a puff of smoke and Eleanor asked, "Would I mind what?"

"Oh, nothing. I was talking to Duchess." I finally caught her, and carried her to the car, placing her inside.

We roared down the road with Duchess screaming 'meow' the whole time, loud enough to nearly split our eardrums.

Eleanor had her hands clasped over her ears. "Holy wow. I didn't know cats could meow that loud. It sure grates on my nerves."

"Mine, too, but I'd feel better having her at the mansion with us. I've heard cats can ward off evil spirits."

"I wondered why you told Sara that your cat has been sick lately. Well, hopefully Duchess can keep the ghosts away."

I highly doubted that would work, but at this point I wasn't all that concerned about ghosts that I didn't feel could hurt me, but a real life murderer was quite another thing.

Before I headed back to the mansion, I flew through the drive-thru at KFC and Ella took our money, asking us where we were going in such a hurry.

"We're overseeing preparations at the Butler Mansion," I said, trying to hold Duchess back from jumping out the opened window.

Eleanor leaned toward the driver's side and added, "We're staying there until the opening."

Ella crossed herself. "You two are nuts. No way would I ever stay at a haunted mansion."

"That's nonsense. That mansion is no more haunted than that lighthouse at the point."

"Yeah, that's also haunted. Good luck to you both, then." Ella slammed the drive thru window in a hurry and she was waving her arms, no doubt retelling the story to her co-workers.

I drove back to the Butler Mansion and saw a van waiting in the parking lot. Two young men were standing outside smoking cigarettes, but another was in a wheelchair.

I wrestled Duchess from the car and made my way for the front door, greeting the men. "Are you the cleaning crew?"

One of the men said, "Yes, and we've been waiting outside in this heat for over half an hour."

"Sorry about that."

"Then why not wait in your van in the air conditioning?" Eleanor asked.

"Air conditioning?" the man in the wheelchair said. "That cheap boss of ours bought a hunk of junk that has no air."

These men sure seemed to have chips on their shoulders already, so I unlocked the door and turned to say, "Make sure you put those cigarette butts in the ashtray by the door here. I don't want the groundskeeper to fuss about picking them off the ground."

They put out the cigarettes and stomped them beneath their feet, not lifting a finger to put them where I requested. If Duchess hadn't been squirming so, I would have given them a piece of my mind.

One of the men carried the man who was wheelchair-bound inside, placing him back in his wheelchair that had been carried inside by the second man. "You need to install a ramp," he grumbled.

"How are you able—?"

He swiveled his chair around, balancing it on only the back wheels for a moment before he rolled his eyes, and spat, "Oh, you're one of those."

"What?"

"You think that just because I'm stuck in this chair that I can't do anything. I assure you I can do my job just fine. There are discrimination laws, you know."

"Sorry. I meant no offense." I crept away while Eleanor gave them instructions on what had to be cleaned and would later meet me in the kitchen.

I sat Duchess down and she darted away. I then pulled out the food from the bags Eleanor had in her arms that she had brought from her house. "I don't care for how those men are speaking to us," I said. "They're making me a little uncomfortable."

"Well, you did insult the man in the wheelchair."

"I didn't mean to. You can't tell me you weren't shocked to see a man in a wheelchair part of a cleaning crew."

"I was, but I know how easily people with handicaps can get offended. I think it's great he wants to work."

After we ate, we retrieved our belongings from the car and made ourselves comfortable in rooms on the second floor. Eleanor's room was opposite mine and while I was alone, the ghost appeared, floating to sit next to me on the bed.

"You're getting me into so much trouble."

She hung her head.

"I'm sorry. I don't mean to offend you, too, but I don't understand why you're here."

The ghost shrugged. Duchess chose that moment to dart into the room, but she skidded to a halt, eyes wide as saucers, as she stared at the ghost who wrapped her arms around me. Duchess then ran from the room, striking her head on the wall outside of the bedroom.

The ghost let me go then and I had to ask, "Are you afraid of cats?" When she nodded, I just had to laugh. "Did you see the ghost here earlier?"

She nodded.

"Did the ghost have anything to do with Katherine's death?"

She shrugged and that brought my spirits down a tad. I had hoped for more clarity, but I suppose if a ghost did have something to do with a murder, it would be mighty hard to prove.

I stretched and made way for Eleanor's room, where she was bouncing on the mattress. "Wow, Agnes. This mattress must be memory foam."

It sure is great, but let's check out the third floor room. I'd feel better if I could assure myself there wasn't a ghost lurking up there."

Eleanor reluctantly followed me, and we carefully went up the narrow stairs that led to the third floor. Once we were back in the small room, I could see the carpet had been replaced with a burgundy area rug. Along one wall was a built-in bookshelf with children's books on the shelves. I stared out the window and saw the cleaning men were bringing in supplies. A truck rumbled into the drive.

"That looks like Bernice," Eleanor said.

Cat Lady was how we knew her the best. She has a slew of cats at her place and she makes some awful moonshine. I couldn't imagine why she'd be here.

Eleanor left the room and out of the corner of my eye, I caught sight of a rocking horse in motion. I turned in a hurry, not willing to let my mind wander right now. My ghost companion motioned with her lips, "Don't look at me."

I left the room in a hurry and made it downstairs, just as Bernice wobbled in the door. "Hello, girls!" she shouted. "Rumor has it that you two were holed up here, and I just had to see it firsthand."

I motioned Bernice through the door that led into the dining room so we would be out of hearing range of the curious looks from the cleaning men who were in the process of dusting.

"Who told you we'd be here?"

Bernice took off her dusty hat and set it on the table, plopping down in a chair. "Well you know ... the senior phone tree. Ella called Elsie, and Elsie called me. Mr. Wilson will be here shortly to check to make sure his sweetheart, Eleanor Mason, is okay."

I smiled tightly. "There certainly has to be something more interesting to talk about in East Tawas today."

Bernice slapped the table with a resounding thump. "Not as interesting as the fixes you girls get yourselves into."

I wasn't about to rise to that barb. "I see. Well, we're simply overseeing the opening of the bed and breakfast on Halloween."

"I see. Is that what all that clamoring is about in the next room?"

"Yes, it's the cleaners."

"Cleaners with big attitudes," Eleanor added. "I sure wish we weren't tied up here at the mansion. We found Katherine Clark's body here yesterday and we haven't even been able to do much in the way of investigating."

"Eleanor, I'm sure Bernice doesn't really want to—"

Bernice rubbed her chin that had several long hairs sprouting from it. "If it's help you girls need, it's help you'll get. Just tell me how I can be of assistance."

Well, I'll be, this might just work. "If you could keep a watch over the cleaning crew, we could leave to check out a few things. I promise we won't be too long."

Eleanor marched through the dining room to the kitchen, opened the refrigerator and peeked inside. "It looks like the fridge is stocked," she said, and she then closed it. "Help yourself to home, just stay out of the way of the cleaning crew. I highly doubt they have much in the way of work ethics."

"Not the way they left cigarette butts outside when I told them to put them in the ashtray outside," I added in irritation.

"Not to worry. I'll set those boys straight if they don't stay on task. What's up with the wheelchair-bound one?"

"He's with the crew and already a bit testy as it is. I'd stay away from him, if I were you."

We left the dining room and gathered the cleaning crew together, introducing Bernice. "She's in charge while we're out."

The man in the wheelchair spat, "Sure, whatever you say, boss." He wheeled away and the other two stared me down until Eleanor took that moment to pull me toward the door.

CHAPTER FIVE

Once we were inside the car, I said, "I just don't like those cleaners. They make me nervous."

"Oh, don't worry about them." She pulled out the mail she had tucked in her purse earlier, examining the return address. Eleanor craned her head in my direction. "Looks like these are all from Jack Winston."

"Jack Winston? As in, resident-dirty-old-man-who-dates-only-young-bimbos?"

"Yup, looks that way. Oh, but if we question him, this is not going to go well. He doesn't even like me."

"Well, he's sure crotchety, but it's the only clue we have to start with. We really need to ask Sara more questions, too, when we see her again. We didn't get a chance to ask how she came to hire Katherine, or if she knew her personally."

"Oh, I doubt that very much since Sara just flew in from Hollywood. She doesn't strike me as the hands-on type of girl."

"That's pretty obvious. All the more reason to dig in deep to solve this case."

I drove up US 23 and merged onto Tawas Beach Road as Eleanor directed me. I came to an abrupt halt when I came to the Tawas Beach Club gate. "Jack lives in a gated community?"

"His son, Henry, does."

"I don't think I've met him before."

"Nope, he lives downstate somewhere, but I heard tell that he bought a house here so that his old man had a place to live. Jack lost his house to one of his ex-wives."

That made me smile, since Jack was kind of a jerk. "How are we going to get in here?"

"Call Martha. Didn't she do realty at one time?"

"Yes. She doesn't any longer, but she might have some connections." I called Martha and she promised to be right over.

Eleanor read a few of the letters. "In these letters, Jack is asking Katherine to meet him, mentioning that it's of great importance."

"Why didn't he just call her?"

"It also says that she keeps ignoring his calls. Why on earth would Jack not just drop by the mansion?"

"Well, if Katherine was blowing him off, maybe he was afraid she might call the law on him."

"True. These letters were mailed to an address in Bay Port, Michigan," Eleanor said.

"So none of those letters were mailed to the Butler Mansion?"

"Nope. Maybe they already connected here in Tawas."

"Perhaps, but I have a feeling that there's more to this story if Jack's involved. Katherine certainly doesn't seem to fit his MO. She wasn't blonde or twenty."

"How on earth do you know how old she was when we only saw her as a corpse?"

"I'm thinking she looks at least thirty."

Eleanor rolled her eyes, but just then, Martha rolled up in her 1970s paneled station wagon. She pulled alongside my car with her windows rolled down. Accompanying her was a shirtless, blond, twenty-something young man who looked surfboard ready.

"It's about time. Do you have the key to get us in?"

"Nope, but Brad here does."

Brad squeezed out of the car, his denim short shorts low on his hips and even my eyes about popped out at the sight. He leaned into my window. "My folks own a place out here."

46

Eleanor's face split into the biggest grin ever. "We appreciate you helping us out."

"I'll escort you to the Winston place. Jack is a riot."

He strode to the fence and opened the gate, then hopped into the back of my car, as did Martha after she parked her wagon on the edge of the road. The car rumbled forward and the gate was then re-locked behind us by a man who waved at Brad.

We drove a few hundred yards and Brad pointed out the driveway that we needed to turn in. I drove up to a gray-sided house that wasn't all that impressive too look at, in my opinion. "Your house looks nicer than this one," I said to Eleanor.

"I bet this one has a much bigger strip of beach than what I have, plus it is part of the Tawas Beach Club."

"Which means what, exactly?"

"Just that not anyone can buy a home here. They have to approve you and check you out first. It's about as high class as Tawas gets."

Most likely, most of them are not from the Tawas area, but I left my thoughts to myself, not wanting to offend Brad. I can't say anything bad about anyone just because they have money. Anyone who works hard deserves whatever he or she can afford. It's not that I think there is anything wrong with high-class people. I'm just a small town person and have always felt uncomfortable around people of means—not that any of them have ever been unkind to me.

When I parked, we all got out and Brad led the way to the door. He explained that we would more likely be allowed in since I had informed him why we were here.

After a few raps, the door was opened by an attractive man with dark hair and a thin mustache, dressed all in white with sandals on his feet. He looked to be about thirty-five. "Hey, Brad. What brings you by?"

"This is Martha, Agnes Barton and Eleanor Mason. They're here to speak with your dad, if he's available."

Henry smiled. "Great, I've been stuck entertaining him all day. At least I can get some work done now."

"Oh, do you work from home?"

"Yes, I'm a writer."

Eleanor's face lit up. "Oh, what kind of book do you write?"

"Spy novels, mostly."

"Oh, how interesting," Eleanor said as she hooked her arm though his. "I love to read. I should try one of your novels sometime."

Instead of yanking his arm away, he played along. "Sure."

Just then, a dark-skinned man joined them. "Quite the lady killer, aren't you, Brad," the man said with a wink.

Henry laughed as Eleanor released his arm. "This is my partner, Tony."

"Oh … oh. How great," I said.

"It's about time he claims me," Tony said. "He's a touch too much *in* the closet."

Henry's hands went to his hips. "I am not. I just don't want to be known as the gay author."

"I can understand that. Well, we won't bother you further if you can point us in the direction of where we might find your father."

We were led outside and Henry waltzed to a lawn chair that was turned away from us, facing Lake Huron, and oh, what a view. The waves pounded the shore now, as the wind had picked us since we were at Eleanor's house and was now quite brisk. There was a dock where a speedboat was moored and I could clearly see the lighthouse on the point that was in the state park.

"It's about time you got away from that confounded computer. You work too much."

"Actually, I haven't been able to work much at all. There are too many distractions around here, lately."

"Perhaps there wouldn't be as many distractions if Tony got a job."

"It has nothing to do with Tony. It's you, Dad. Why don't you call one of your lady friends over?"

"I don't have a steady flow of women since you've locked up nearly all of my assets."

"I had to or you'd be broke by now. You can't stay in a spending frenzy your entire life."

"I'd rather spend my wad then leave it for you boys to fight over when I'm gone."

"Sorry," Henry said to us. "Dad, you have company."

The ghost floated over to where we were, moving to a lawn chair next to Jack. We walked around to where Jack could see us. "Hiya, Jack."

He rolled his eyes and pounded the arms of his chair with a thump. "Oh, great. What do you people want?"

Martha's wild hair blew in the wind as she clung to Brad's arm. "Maybe we better leave you investigators to your questioning," she said as Brad led her away.

He sat upright. "Questioning? What in tarnation do you have to question me about?"

"Can I have a seat? Eleanor asked. I'm about ready to fall over in this heat."

"Suit yourself, fish lady."

I waved my arms frantically. "Not that chair, Eleanor!"

Just before Eleanor completely sat on the ghost, she flew up and away.

"What are you carrying on about? I have sat next to Jack before without incident."

"Oh, never mind. There was a bee in the chair but it flew away," I grumbled, feeling like a complete fool now. I plopped down in a chair opposite Jack, and then said, "Do you know Katherine Clark?"

His eyes widened. "Katherine?"

"Yes, the woman who met a premature death at the Butler Mansion yesterday."

He began breathing hard, his eyes filling with tears and he swiped at them with his hands. "Katherine—dead?"

Oh, no. "I'm sorry. I thought you already knew."

"No, I didn't. They said on the news that they found a body at the Butler Mansion, but didn't release any names yet."

I felt so bad. "I'm sorry, Jack. How did you know her?"

He swiped at his large nose with a hand. "I'd rather not say, especially to the two of you."

Can't say I blame him for that. "We really want to find out who might have murdered Katherine, and if you're gonna react like this, then I'd think you'd want that, too."

Jack clamped his jaw tightly closed, his lower lip protruding. His brown eyes shifted from me to a shadow behind me. I whirled as Henry now stood behind me, holding a tray of lemonade. "I brought you some refreshments." He set the tray down and asked, "What's the matter, Dad?"

"Nothing, son. Run along and work on your book. They brought me bad news and it's nothing for you to concern yourself with."

Henry's brow arched. "Are you sure? Because you really look upset."

"I'm sure, son."

Henry reluctantly left and I had the strangest urge to take ahold of Jack's hand and couldn't stop myself, but when I did, he slapped my hand away. "What in tarnation are you trying to do? You're so not my type."

I sighed. "Sorry, I just felt bad and I wanted to ... oh, I don't know what I was trying to do."

"You were taking leave of your senses," Eleanor added. "You know Jack only is interested in barely-eighteen-year-old girls."

"Hogwash," Jack sputtered. "I'm not who you think I am," he blubbered. "All those women who were with me, I paid them to accompany me around town."

"Like… in … hookers?" Eleanor asked.

"No, I never touched any of them. I have had eyes only for Elsie Bradford all these years, but trying to get close to that woman is like pulling whatever teeth I have left in my mouth."

I had to agree with that, and frankly, I was shocked by this revelation. "You never know unless you try."

"Believe me, that ship has passed."

"So what about Katherine? How long were you sending her letters?"

"I-I wasn't."

Eleanor produced the letters and Jack's face reddened to a deep purple. "How did you get these? They're private."

"We found them in Katherine's belongings. Why was it so important that you speak with her?"

"I'm not saying a word."

I stood. "Okay, I'll have to make sure Sheriff Peterson gets these letters, then. It would think you would rather tell us than be questioned by the sheriff."

"And if I tell you what you want to know, do you promise not to turn those letters over to the fuzz?"

I couldn't promise, but I didn't want to let him know that. "Eleanor and I plan to investigate this case out of the eye of law enforcement, if that makes you happy."

He held out his hand. "How about you just give me the letters to assure that the sheriff never sees them? He might just get the wrong idea."

"What kind of idea is that? I must admit that these letters sure put you on the hot seat. You seemed desperate to see Katherine in person."

His arm dropped and the ghost hovered by in encouragement.

"Yes, I was quite desperate, but not how you might think. I wasn't dating her or even trying to."

"So why was it so important to see her?" Eleanor asked.

"You probably overheard Henry and me talking. He's taken nearly all of my money for safekeeping and only gives me a few hundred a week for spending money."

"What gives him the right to do that?"

"Well, I'm a spender, but those women don't accompany me for free. They cost me like a five hundred a week."

"Then there are the winters in Florida," I said. "I bet that cost you a bundle, too."

"Yup, but that gold-digger I married last year really took me to the cleaners."

"I didn't even know you were married."

"Yes, well, anyway, after that fiasco, I agreed to hand over my bank account to my son and I had no idea at the time that he'd keep me on such a short leash financially. That's when I met Katherine. She told me about this financial opportunity, but after I managed to sneak away twenty thousand from Henry and handed over the cash to Katherine, she quit answering my phone calls and didn't return any of my messages."

"And she was living in Bay Port?"

"Yes, I didn't even know she had come to the Tawas area until a few weeks ago when I ran into her at Walmart."

"What happened? Did she tell you why she hadn't called you back?"

"No, she threatened to call the law on me if I ever set foot near her again."

I plopped down in my chair and the ghost crossed her arms, obviously as irritated as I was. "So she swindled you out of twenty thousand?"

"Yup. It's no wonder my son keeps my funds locked up. I really never thought she'd do that to me. I had thought that if I allowed her some time, then I'd ask her if she actually invested the money, or outright stole it from me in some kind of scheme."

"Why did you trust her anyway?"

"I don't know. I overheard her talking to a customer at the Bay Port Inn about an investment tip she got from her stockbroker brother."

"What was the investment in?"

"Solar technology, an outfit called International Energy. It sounded like green technology that would be all the rage these days. I expected to get in on the ground floor and she told me I had bought fifty percent of the stock."

"Which would net you quite a sum if it went global."

"Yes. Katherine told me that they were expanding business in the South that would really put them on the map financially. You know, everyone these days is all about green. If they had only planned to do business in the North I would never have handed off the money, but the South has far more sunlight than we get up here so I figured it was a sweet deal."

"Why would you even trust someone you didn't know like that?"

"She was so convincing and I had to do something to increase my cash flow."

"How did you get the money from your son?"

"I took it without his knowledge. I still don't think he knows it's gone, but when he does, it's gonna be World War III around here. He might seem calm enough now, but don't be fooled. There is plenty of Jack Winston in him."

"And you never planned to harm Katherine after she swindled you?"

"Of course I did. That's a pretty normal reaction. Now that she's dead, I'll for sure never get my money back."

Jack's eyes widened, but I didn't pay any attention to what that was all about as I suggested, "It might be better if you told your son the truth about the money before he finds out."

"What money?" Henry asked from behind me.

I whirled and said, "Geez, don't you know you shouldn't be sneaking up on old folks like that. You gave me a near heart attack."

Henry pursed his lips. "How else do you think I find out about what the old man is up to?" He crossed his arms.

"Confound it. You're sneakier than a snake, Henry. Okay, I might as well up and tell you that I found your checkbook and wrote myself a check for twenty thousand a few months back," Jack admitted.

Henry's eyes narrowed to slits. "Why on earth did you need that kind of money?"

"I ran into what I thought was a great investment, but it looks like I got swindled, and now as it turns out, that woman, Katherine Clark was found dead at the Butler Mansion," Jack said somberly. "She was the one I gave the money to."

"What kind of investment, exactly?"

"A solar technology company, International Energy. Katherine told me I was getting in on the ground floor and would be getting a fifty percent interest in the company. They were planning to expand into the South, even. Sounded like a good deal at the time."

"Why on earth did you do that, Dad?"

"You're barely giving me enough money to get by with."

"Two hundred a week isn't much for Jack. He's used to living the highlife," Eleanor said.

"Well, I just didn't want to see him throwing all of his cash at those bimbos." Henry's shoulders drooped a bit now. "Is there any way we can get the money back?"

"That's where we come in," I began. "We need to find out if Katherine still had the money, or if someone else was also involved in her scheme."

"I just don't understand why she came to town or took a job at the Butler Mansion," Eleanor said. "Why turn up in the same town where the man lived that you swindled?"

"Unless she was sure that Jack wouldn't call the cops," I said.

"At what point did you realize that she took your money Jack, or did you?"

"I still believed I could at least get my money back if she'd only speak to me."

"You still thought that after she threatened you?"

Jack took a drink of his lemonade, and then said, "Well, I guess I just didn't want to believe it. Agnes, maybe if you and Eleanor dig into Katherine's death, you might just find the money."

"If it's in her bank accounts there might be a money trail. Did you write the check to her for the twenty thousand?"

"No, I wrote it to myself. Katherine insisted she get the money in cash. That way she'd be able to buy the stock right away. With a sizable check you'd have to wait ten days for it to clear the bank."

Eleanor bobbed her head. "He's right, Agnes. You'd have to wait with a check."

"I'd sure like to know if this International Energy is a real company or a dummy corporation set up to look authentic for an elaborate scheme."

"If that's the case, Aggie, that Katherine might have swindled more folks in town."

"Exactly, and I can't help but think that she targeted senior citizens, which really makes me sick to my stomach."

"Sounds like you ladies have a case to unravel," Henry said. "Come inside, Dad, and we'll go over your finances. The last thing I want you to think is that I'm trying to take your money. I just don't want to see you go broke."

CHAPTER SIX

We walked through the house to where Martha sat next to Brad, who was in an in-depth conversation about the best surfing beaches with Tony. When Martha spotted us, she said, "Oh, Mother. Give me a ride back to my car."

Brad barely looked up, and when she wasn't able to even get him to look up at her when she announced she was leaving, she stomped off toward the door with us in tow.

When we were back in the car and I was backing up, Eleanor turned to look at Martha in the backseat. "Brad seems nice, but is he—"

Martha sighed. "Probably. I sure know how to pick them."

Eleanor faced the front again. "Oh, don't be too hard on yourself. I'm sure you'll find a new one on the beach later."

That was classic Martha. She liked young men and had a healthy supply. Even though she was forty, she was quite shapely and dressed provocatively most days. Cat suits were her favorite piece of apparel. She did have a gig at the local realty office once, but she's not a conformist. She instead prefers to live for free in my Winnebago that has been parked at the Tawas campground next to the pier.

"How about after we drop you at your car, we follow you back to the campground?"

"Sure, I can throw something on the grill."

"But shouldn't we get back to the mansion soon?" Eleanor asked.

"We will, but I'm sure Bernice is overseeing things just fine."

The man who had closed it behind us earlier opened the gate, and Martha hopped out on the other side and followed us to the campground. I glanced in the back seat to assure myself that my ghost partner was still with me and she was, but staring out the window.

"Why do you keep looking back there, Agnes?" Eleanor wanted to know. "You've been doing that a lot lately. Is there something you're not telling me?"

I gripped the steering wheel and laughed nervously. "Whatever do you mean by that?"

"Ever since the accident, you seem a bit off-kilter, is all."

"Well, I did rattle my head."

"People change sometimes after an accident. How have you been feeling, really?"

"I've had some headaches. That's why I had a CT scan yesterday."

"Did you get the results?"

"You know, I never did. I'm sure if there were any problems, Dr. Thomas would have told me."

I made the turn into the campground and parked alongside my Winnebago where a group of young men were sitting on the picnic table, all of them wearing cutoff shorts.

"I've never seen so many bare-chested men in my life," Eleanor said. "It looks like it won't be long before Martha has herself a new beau."

"Nothing new there, but just why are these men here when Martha isn't?"

"Not sure, but looks like she's not too upset about it," Eleanor pointed out as Martha raced from her car that she parked in a hurry to greet the men.

Eleanor and I struggled out of the car, which made me believe that Eleanor was about as tired as I was. It had already been a long day. While Eleanor made her way to the group of young men, I stopped and looked across the way, where the black monstrosity of a trailer stood with thick drapes covering the windows like usual.

Leotyne Williams rolled into East Tawas a while ago and hasn't left yet. Eleanor and I have also called her a gypsy, on account of she lives in a trailer and is of Romanian descent. Of course, early on we also thought she was a witch. I think it had something to with the fact that she has long, stringy hair and wears long black dresses despite the heat. The ghost floated nearby, and instead of joining Martha and Eleanor, it might be the time to ask Leotyne to look into that crystal ball of hers, since she's known to be a clairvoyant. She's also given me advice in the past, but it's usually sketchy at best. More like a riddle than anything else, but it's always rung true, so I have learned to take her advice.

I rapped on the door and the ghost bobbed next to me when Anna Parsons opened it. I had met Anna in the hospital on one of my numerous overnight stays there. Leotyne took Anna in not long ago when she needed a place to stay and Anna is Leotyne's apprentice.

"Hello," I said as I clambered up the steps of the trailer and Anna raced out of the way, pressing herself to the wall of the kitchenette.

Before I had time to ask if Leotyne was here, I jerked my head sideways as an earth-shattering scream coming from Leotyne echoed in the trailer. My ghost companion was also quite frightened and her mouth was wide open in a screaming motion, too. She formed a black mist that flew into one wall of the trailer after the other, sending books flying to the floor. Leotyne grabbed a broom and began to swing wildly at the mist and I shouted, "Stop it! You're scaring her."

Leotyne stopped mid-swipe. "Scaring her? She's wrecking the place."

"That's because you were screaming."

Leotyne put the broom down. "Why'd you bring a ghost into my trailer for?"

"It's okay, I won't let her hurt you," I cooed to the ghost that appeared in silhouette form now, her chest rising and falling. She then threw her ghostly arms around me and I hugged the air lightly since if I did it too hard, my arms would go straight through her. Or that was my reasoning, since this was *way* bazaar.

Leotyne smoothed her hair and straightened her clothing now, motioning Anna to join her at the table. "It's okay, dear, the ghost is with her."

Anna raced over and sat down, her eyes round and wide. "I-I didn't think gh-ghosts were real."

"Of all the crazy things for someone to say that proclaims herself as clairvoyant. Of course they're real," I said as I sat opposite them and the ghost floated close by. "I'm staying at the Butler Mansion and I can tell you that I've seen one there, too. Or I should say, Eleanor and I did." I pursed my lips since I had to tell them the whole story. At least someone besides me could see the ghost now. "Not sure if you were aware of it or not, but I had an accident where I suffered quite the concussion, and when I woke up this ghost was there and has been with me ever since."

Leotyne leaned forward, her eyes squinty. "Don't be too hard on the girl, she's learning. So it's attached itself to you, then. When was the first time you saw the ghost?"

"In the hospital."

Leotyne's fingers tapped the table. "Interesting. So it had nothing to do with the body that was discovered at the Butler Mansion that they spoke about on the news?"

"Not that I'm aware of."

Leotyne fingered her crystal ball thoughtfully. "The ghost isn't the same person who died at the mansion recently, but it's a bit foggy. She's attached to you for some reason and I'm not so convinced that it was at the hospital for sure, but you could ask around. I expect if someone has seen a ghost at the hospital before, they might tell you. Maybe."

That really didn't help much. "They might think I'm off my rocker, too."

"You are that, Agnes. Have your partner, Eleanor, ask the questions, since she's perceived as a brick short of a full load already."

I frowned. "Oh, come on. Eleanor might be a little impulsive, but she's more sane than most. I can't ask her to do that without telling her the whole story."

"You mean she doesn't also see the ghost?" Anna asked.

"No, and she doesn't know I see one, either. It's so hard to keep this all to myself."

"Yes, it's important not to tell anyone, but you do need to figure out who she is at some point. Ghosts often want something and you need to figure out what it is."

I pointed out the crystal ball. "Can't you see something in that globe of yours that might help?"

Leotyne looked into the crystal ball and shook her head. "It's all fogged up."

"Let me try," Anna said. She then leaned toward the globe, putting her fingers on it. "Yes, all fogged up. She might not want us to tell you who she really is."

The ghost shook her head.

"Do you even know who you really are?" I asked the ghost. When she only shrugged, I added, "I just don't understand. Can either of you at least tell me something about the woman who died at the mansion, Katherine Clark?"

Leotyne once again looked into her ball. "Beware of the three o'clock hour." She then stared at me. "It's not safe for you to stay at the mansion. It's a very dangerous place, with many angry spirits."

"Why angry?"

"That's all I see."

"Anna, you try, please. I have to know."

Anna smiled sadly. "Sorry, that's all there is to know. Try back in a few days and maybe we can see something more."

I stood up, more aggravated than ever, just as Eleanor waltzed into the trailer. When she spotted me, she clutched her chest. "Oh, thank the heavens above. I was so scared when I couldn't find you."

"Oh, come now. You had to have known I'd be here."

Eleanor's eyes darted around nervously. "I suppose. Hello, Leotyne. Where's your hellhounds?"

"I had only one hound and he's met an unfortunate end."

I gulped. "Run over by a car?"

"Nope, old age. Let me just say that he was an old dog."

"What did she tell you?" asked Eleanor.

"Nothing much. You know, another riddle: 'Beware the three o'clock hour' and something about 'the mansion being dangerous.'"

"I knew it. We shouldn't be there."

"Well, we're not there right now, so don't worry. I'm not about to be chased from the mansion … not in this case. Let's go."

Eleanor and I made our way back to where Martha was turning hot dogs with a fork on her grill. "About time you turned up, Mother. I was about ready to gather together a search party."

Just then, a trashcan was tipped over as a ferocious bark was heard. It came from Leotyne's dearly departed hellhound that was now in ghostly form, chasing my ghost up a nearby tree.

"What on earth," Eleanor began. "What tipped that trash can over?"

"Oh, probably a squirrel."

"I didn't see any squirrel."

"W-Well, you know it must have darted away fast, is all."

"Hot dogs or no hot dogs?" Martha asked as she tapped her fork on the grill to get our attention.

"Sure, I'm starving."

Soon we were all digging in and the men left to go swimming, informing us they had already eaten. They laughed when I told them to wait an hour after they ate to go swimming.

"So what's your case about?"

I quickly gave Martha a run-down about how Eleanor and I had found yet another body and what Jack had told us."

"Wow, you two sure manage to find a lot of bodies. It's like your specialty."

Between bites, Eleanor asked me, "Do you think Jack offed Katherine?"

"You know, I'm not sure. He sure had reason to, but he seemed to believe that he might just get that money back."

"I know, but there was nothing stopping him from showing up at the mansion and choking Katherine silly."

"I'm aware of that, but Jack seemed pretty upset that she's dead. I think he's come to the realization that he'll never get his money back. At least his son wasn't all that upset about the missing money."

"Well, it was Jack's money from the sounds of it. I just would hate for my son to show up one day and try to take my purse strings."

"From the sounds of it, Jack had agreed to allow his son to do that."

"Yes, well, he wasn't too happy about being kept on that short of a financial leash."

"True, but boy, Jack sure wasn't the man I thought he was."

"I'm wondering about that. Other than calling me fish lady once, he wasn't himself at all. He's never been kind to either of us."

"People sometimes do put up fronts."

"I've known him longer than you and I'm telling you, I'm just not buying his calm demeanor. He's on the top of my suspect list as far as I'm concerned."

"We really need to find out if there really is an International Energy. I can't think that Jack would come up with an elaborate story like that."

"I'm not saying he made up that part, just that his temper might have gotten the best of him when she swindled him. I can *so* see Jack throttling that woman."

I could too, actually. "We need more proof than that. We need to find out if Katherine might have had an accomplice, or if anyone else in town had been taken to the cleaners by her."

"Most seniors we know don't have the kind of money to invest like that."

"Elsie Bradford does, but I don't really understand why senior citizens need to invest their money. It's not like they need a ton to enjoy their lives."

"That's true, but not everyone has much at all. Many of them are barely making do on their social security checks. Not really the type of folks who can afford to invest money at all."

"We need to do some checking around, and soon."

"Hopefully, by that you mean tomorrow, because I've about had it for today," Eleanor admitted.

"Believe me, I know it." I stood and stretched and asked Martha, "What's up with your brother? I haven't seen Stuart since he left my house in a rush the other day. I sure hope he hasn't left town."

Martha rubbed a cloth over the picnic table, cleaning it. "Stuart? Well, he's been busy, I guess."

My hands went to my hips and I demanded, "Do you know where he is or not?"

She shrugged. "I have more important things to do than worry about Stuart."

"Like lounging on the beach all day?" Eleanor asked.

Martha smiled kindly. "You know yourself, Eleanor, that you'd rather be doing that instead of hanging around with my mom all the time."

"I don't hang around with your mother all the time, but actually we're in charge of getting the Butler Mansion ready for the opening on Halloween."

Martha clapped her hands together. "That sounds splendid. Are you planning to make the place look all Halloweenie inside?"

I made a face at the ghost who was still up a tree with the howling ghost dog below. Since nobody reacted to hearing the beast, I just had to wonder if it was all in my head. Then again, why was I able to hear the dog barking, but I couldn't understand a word the ghost said?

"Are you okay, Mother?" Martha asked.

I snapped my neck around and sputtered, "Y-Yes, I'm fine. Why?"

"Well, for one thing you keep making faces at that tree over there. Is there something over there that you see, but we don't?"

"Yeah, Aggie? Is there?" Eleanor also wanted to know.

They both had the most peculiar expression on their faces and I knew they must be worried, so I laughed it off. "For a moment, there were a couple of squirrels, is all. Ever since my accident, my mind sure has been wandering."

"Yes, like right out of your head. You better give that Dr. Thomas a call to see how your CT scan turned out," Eleanor suggested.

I made the requested quick call to appease the two of them, and Dr. Thomas' nurse told me everything checked out fine. When I hung up, I asked Martha, "Would you mind entertaining Eleanor for a few hours? The doctor wants to see me," I lied.

"I'll go with you, Agnes. I insist."

"Come on, Eleanor. I'd really rather go alone. You could lounge at the beach while I'm gone."

Martha grinned. "That sounds great. Come on, Eleanor, I'll introduce you around."

"Okay, but remember, I'm engaged to Mr. Wilson."

"That doesn't mean you can't look, dear."

I got into the car and headed straight to the hospital, not to see Dr. Thomas, but to question the staff about the presence of ghosts there. The ghost floated down into the passenger's seat while the ghost dog chased after our car all the way to US 23 before he gave up.

"Whew, I didn't think we'd ever lose that dog." The ghost bobbed her head in agreement and I asked her, "Are you sure you can't speak?"

She shook her head in response.

"Weird. How come that dog can bark, then?"

She shrugged and I gripped the wheel hard as I turned toward the hospital. "I'm going to ask around at the hospital to see if anyone knows who you are."

The ghost shook her head.

"I saw you in the hospital the first time."

She shook her head again. Fog then appeared on the inside of the windshield and the letters appeared that read '1930.'

"You died in 1930?"

The ghost nodded.

"Why did you attach yourself to me?"

She pounded her head and more letters were scribbled into the fogged window, 'murder.'

"So you were murdered in 1930?"

The ghost bounced on the seat in excitement.

"Okay, so you want me to find out who murdered you?"

'No,' was scrawled into the fog and then, 'help you.'

"So you were murdered in 1930, but you want to help me in my investigation?"

The fog writing disappeared and was replaced with the word, 'investigations.'

I skidded to a stop at the red light and my heart pounded in my chest. "If you were murdered, I suppose that whoever did the deed might just be dead now, right?"

She nodded her head.

I clammed up now. I had hoped to find out a little more about her than that. Not only has this ghost now attached to me, but also fancied herself an investigator.

I advanced through the intersection as I asked, "What is your name?"

"Caroline," she said.

I crashed over the curb in disbelief when the ghost finally spoke. I had my head on the steering wheel when my door was opened with a concerned Trooper Sales searching me for injuries. "Are you okay, Agnes?"

"Y-Yes," I choked out. "I really made a mess of things," I added as I got out of the car.

He stared at where I had run over the curb. "It looks fine. Did you have a spell or something?"

"Day-dreaming I suppose."

"Well, if you're sure you're okay, just drive off the curb and go about your business."

I nodded and did just that, making way back toward the campground since I didn't have to question anyone at the hospital about if they had seen a ghost. I now knew her name was Caroline and not much else. I'd like to have questioned her further, but when Trooper Sales showed up, she disappeared. Not what I'd call the best of investigators, but hopefully I'd be able to find out more about her later. Since she was able to say her name, I hoped she could share more about who she really was, and just who might have murdered her. If not, I guessed I was okay with her helping me out with our investigation. So far, she had proved useful opening doors. The one thing I wasn't so sure about was if I should tell Eleanor about our secret partner.

Chapter Seven

As I drove by the city beach, I couldn't help notice a Ninja motorcycle, like the one I had seen Stuart tool off in just the other day, and in a hurry, no less.

I pulled up next to his bike and made my way slowly, keeping an eye out for Stuart. Something told me he was doing something besides enjoying the view on Lake Huron.

There was a yellow tarp fashioned into a tent with the word 'danger' printed on it, and that told me one of two things: there were either bare wires under that tarp, or it would be the perfect place to spy on someone. Since I believed Stuart's absence from my life had nothing to do with him being a history major or even studying ancient civilizations, I took a look-see under that tent.

I was quiet as a mouse, or so I thought, but Stuart's body stiffened and he turned, his eyes widening upon locking eyes with me. One hand was still on a binocular-looking thing that was attached to a tripod, the other on a handle of a Glock pistol stuck into the waistband of his pants.

He pulled me into the tent and before I had a chance to say anything, he hissed from between his teeth, "What are you doing here?"

"I saw your bike and figured out this might be where you were hiding out. Who are you spying on?"

"I can't tell you. Go back to your car, slowly, and forget you ever saw me."

"What are you up to? This certainly doesn't look like you're studying ancient civilizations to me."

He shook his head, taking another look through the spyglass. That's it, is he a— "Are you a spy, Stuart?"

"Spy? No! You really need to get out of here before you blow my cover. Damn, he's gone now."

"Who's gone?"

The flap of the tent came up and a man holding a revolver strode in, pointing the gun at me. "Who's the dame?"

I stared at the man who was about my age, his gray hair quite short, wire rimmed-glasses on his face. Not only was he thin, but muscular—and quite short in stature, too.

"I don't think I like the sound of that. Who uses names like dames these days? Who are you, anyway?"

"The name's Len McGroovy."

I laughed. "That's one of the worst names I have ever heard in the whole creation of bad cover names."

"Put that gun down, Len. That's my mother."

"Is she a special agent, too?"

"No, and let's keep this between us."

"I've been in retirement a whole two weeks and here you are ruining it."

Oh, wow. I have run smack dab into some real spy-level stuff here. Or whatever was going on. "I'll be leaving now. You two can work out your differences after I leave."

"You should have thought about that before," Len said. "Out, the both of you." Stuart and I were led outside and into the back of a rustic black van where Stuart was relieved of his firearm.

As the van backed up, I had to say, "Smart move about using an old van. A brand new one would be so much more suspect."

A woman climbed in behind us and laughed when she spotted me. "Still having problems with working with others, Stuart?"

"I'm his mother," I announced. I gripped my purse tightly. "I sure hope you can drop me off at the campground. My best friend is searching for me by now. Did I mention that my granddaughter is married to a state trooper? Stuart's dad was also a—"

The woman covered her ears. "No wonder you joined the FBI. I would to get away from a mother like that, too."

I wanted to give her long black hair a hard yank. "I bet you never call your mother."

"Say one more word, Granny, and I'll pop you."

I smiled and whipped her with my handbag, she then tumbled over and Stuart wrestled her gun from her hands. Len looked in the rearview mirror and stomped on the gas.

Stuart opened the side door and gave me a gentle shove from the careening van. I tumbled to the soft grass since the van had only started to gain speed, and Stuart landed nearby.

"What do you have in that bag of yours, Mother?"

"Rolled change. I was planning to drop it off at the bank."

"Looks like you lost your bag."

"That's okay."

"But now they'll know where you live."

"I'm staying at the Butler Mansion for a few days. Hopefully, that will give you plenty of time to clear your business up with Len and that lady. Who was she, anyway?"

Stuart walked me to my car. "Oh, her? She's my wife."

"Well, that sure explains things. I don't suppose you'll tell me what you're doing."

"I can't, really, but now my cover is blown and I'll be lucky if I find them again."

"If I can be any more help, let me know."

"You can do plenty if you stay away from me for the time being. I'll have to go into deep cover now."

I tried to say be careful, but he jogged toward the beach,

disappearing. Two black cars pulled into the parking lot and I took my leave before I got into more trouble.

When I pulled back into the campground, I parked next to my Winnebago and hurried for the beach with my ghost finally appearing next to me.

"Where were you when I was in trouble?"

"I was there, but I was too scared to appear to you. I hate guns," Caroline said.

"Thanks for nothing, but I suppose it doesn't matter. I just wish I knew what Stuart is really doing."

"Don't you already have an important case to figure out?"

I sighed. Now I had two partners to answer to. "Yes, if I can get Eleanor off the beach."

"Who are you talking to?" Eleanor asked walking up.

"Just talking out loud, is all," I said, more quickly than I had intended.

Her arms folded across her chest. "Did you know Dr. Thomas was at the beach today?"

Oh, no. "Oh, so that's why he wasn't at the hospital when I got there."

"Don't you dare give me a line of malarkey like that, Agnes. What's really going on?"

I pulled at the neck of my shirt. "Oh, well ... you see, I just had to find Stuart. He's up to something and I just don't know what."

"You lied to me once today already, Agnes. Do you really think I'll buy some lame story about Stuart now? I suppose the next thing you'll come up with is that you were kidnapped by some goon that Stuart was watching."

The ghost Caroline chuckled. "She got you there, Agnes,"

"No, of course not! That sounds ludicrous." Not any more than what really had happened.

I gazed over at the ghost and for a moment and I almost spilled my guts, but I just wasn't ready for *that* conversation yet. "Okay, fine then. All I know is that we had better get back to the Butler Mansion before Sara Knoxville finds out we're not there." I bit my pinkie finger, and then added, "I sure hope Bernice is making sure the cleaners are doing their work. Halloween is coming up pretty fast now."

"Fine, I'll let this drop for now, but I'm going to get to the bottom of what's really going on with you or my name isn't Eleanor Mason." Eleanor stomped over to the car and I climbed behind the wheel as the ghost faded away in the bright sunlight. It's just as well, since I couldn't very well talk to the ghost, Caroline, and Eleanor at the same time.

I tooled back to the Butler Mansion at last, lowering myself in my seat when I passed what I thought were Andrew and Sara coming toward us on US 23. "Oh, drat," I said.

Eleanor was equally low in her seat. "That was Andrew and Sara, wasn't it?"

"Yup. I'm fairly certain it was."

"Then you had better floor it, Aggie, before they find out we skipped out of the mansion when we were supposed to stay there."

I jerked the wheel, barely making the turn, and skidded to a stop at the mansion—my eyes about popped outta my head at the felines that now strutted across the yard. "Strange, I don't remember that many cats being here when we left."

Eleanor chuckled. "Well, it certainly looks like there's plenty here now."

I climbed out of the car, feeling my nagging hip even more since Stuart had pushed me out of a moving van. There were certainly more cats here than there were before we left earlier. "That Bernice sure has some explaining to do."

We climbed the few steps and when we stomped through the door, Bernice said, "Don't blame me. I tried to tell them to get back to work." She was trying to explain why the cleaners were lounging around drinking lemonade, noticeable from the tart lemon fragrance in the air.

"I don't care about that. Why are there so many blasted cats here?"

"Yeah, like way more than when we left," Eleanor added. "There have to be, like, twenty cats outside."

Bernice began to rub her hands. "I suspect my cats followed me here. It's not all that far away."

"Well, please get them out of here before Sara finds out."

"Before Sara finds out what?" Sara asked from the doorway with Andrew standing next to her, an unreadable expression on his face.

"Just that cats seem to be all over the place outside," I explained.

"Nothing wrong with a few cats, I suppose, but we don't need quite so many roaming the property," Sara said.

Andrew cleared his throat. "How is the cleaning going, Agnes?"

"I-I'm not sure."

"And would that be because you weren't here?"

"We left for a few hours. Bernice was left in charge."

Sara stared up toward the ceiling. "It looks like there's still quite a bit of cleaning to be done. Perhaps I shouldn't have asked you and Eleanor to oversee things."

"Not at all. We just had to—"

"Buy more lemonade," Bernice added. "Just in time for their break."

"From the looks of it, they've been on break all day," Eleanor said. "Get moving boys," she clapped her hands. "Chop, chop."

The men dashed off with huge smiles on their faces, obviously star struck from being in the same room with an actress of Sara Knoxville's caliber.

I went into the next room and Andrew followed closely behind. He leaned a hand on the back of a chair, and asked, "Where did you go?"

74

"We're looking into the investigation of Katherine Clark's death, of course. Eleanor and I found letters from Jack Winston to her."

Andrew's eyes narrowed slightly, "Oh, really? This I have to hear."

I gave Andrew the rundown about how Katherine had scammed Jack, and how he still had hoped he'd get his money back.

"Sure sounds like Katherine was up to no good. Scams on the elderly are nothing new, either. It seems like Jack would be smart enough not to take financial advice from a complete stranger."

"That's what I thought, but his son, Henry, kept him on a short leash financially."

"That's understandable, since Jack is known to drop quite the amount of cash."

I then told Andrew how it had been agreed upon and how Jack had cashed a check for twenty thousand.

"Do you think Jack is responsible for Katherine's murder?"

"Not really, but I can't say for positive. He did seem awfully upset when we told him Katherine had been murdered. At the time, it never occurred to me that they hadn't released her name on the news yet."

"So what about the letters? Are you planning to turn them over to the sheriff?"

"Actually, not just yet. I want to figure out what really happened to Katherine first."

Andrew nodded. "Okay, but make sure this place is cleaned from top to bottom. I'll keep Sara busy while you conduct your investigation, but remember, Halloween is tomorrow. Sara has visitors coming from Hollywood for the grand opening."

Duchess skidded into the dining room, staring at the wall like something was there—something unseen by me. I picked her up and gave her a good petting until a black mist formed in the corner of the room. It was then that I squeezed poor Duchess hard enough to cause her to meow loudly. I backed away as a man formed in the mist, placed a finger against his lips, and disappeared through the opposite wall.

Caroline appeared, darting hastily after the mist, shouting, "Don't you dare walk away from me," and disappearing through the wall in pursuit.

I shook my head in disbelief. The house was much more haunted that I had thought. First, there was a woman Eleanor and I had followed up the stairs and now a man that was sneaking around. Caroline's pursuit of the man seemed even more peculiar. Had she known this man when she was alive? Finding out the truth about Caroline took center stage now. I had hoped I'd be able to gain more information, but why did I have the sneaking suspicion that there was more to Caroline's death than met the eye, and that it was directly related to this mansion?

Chapter Eight

Sara hung around for a half-hour longer, and the cleaners did more work in that half-hour than they probably had the entire day. She was standing in the yard when a truck rumbled up the drive and Eleanor swept the porch in a hurry. We then watched while pumpkins were unloaded and stacked around the porch.

"I hope you don't mind carving pumpkins," Sara said with a smile.

"Of course not," I said, but my insides just cringed as I realized just how many pumpkins were arranged on the porch.

Sara waved as Andrew led her to his SUV, and I sunk onto a wicker rocking chair on the porch. "I can't believe she expects us to carve pumpkins."

Eleanor's brow rose. "What's wrong with that?"

"Nothing, if there weren't, like, fifty of them."

"Just imagine all of those pumpkins lit up on Halloween night, Agnes. It will look so great when the trick or treater's show up."

"If we ever get this mansion ready in time."

"We will. The cleaners have been working much harder since Sara came."

A stream of cars came up the drive next, and Mr. Wilson was helped out of one, his rolling walker handed to him by his granddaughter, Millicent. When she carried plastic bags that swayed as she walked, I dreaded the obvious. Mr. Wilson had bought groceries that would most likely be ingredients for his tuna casserole.

Not a bad dish if you cared for tuna fish, but not all that good since I had already eaten it hundreds of times before.

I smiled weakly. "Hello, Wilson. Fancy seeing you here."

Millicent smiled in greeting. "I tried to tell grandpa that we'd probably get in your way since you're responsible for readying the mansion for the opening, but he insisted we help you out. I think he misses Eleanor," she whispered in my ear as she passed from the porch into the mansion.

Millicent looked around, and instead of pointing out what needed to be cleaned, she waltzed over to the fireplace that had grotesque figurines and faces carved into the mantle. "Wow," she began. "This looks like something you'd see in some Boris Karloff movie."

"My thoughts exactly, and I can't help but wonder if this place is haunted for real," I added.

"Probably might be since Grandpa told me about the history of the place. This old place dates back to 1859, four years after Tawas was founded."

My brow shot up on account of the fact that Millicent wasn't from the Tawas area. "Are you some kind of history buff?" I asked.

"Oh, I love history, and I have always loved the Tawas area, but actually the Butler Mansion is really more in the Tadium area."

Eleanor joined us, volunteering to put the groceries away. Once she was out of sight and Mr. Wilson was settled in a wing back chair near the fireplace, I asked, "I don't suppose you know, Mr. Wilson, about the goings on around Tawas back in the 30s?"

"I suppose not, since I was born in '32."

"What would you like to know, Agnes?" Millicent asked. "I'd be happy to help out."

"That would be nice. I'm actually wondering about a woman by the name of Caroline. I don't have a last name and she died sometime around 1930. She might have been a victim of a crime, or died in a traffic accident in Tawas."

A notebook appeared in Millicent's hand and she jotted down the name and year, circling it in red. "I'll be happy to do some checking. I'll see if the library has any microfiche lying around."

"You won't find any microfiche in the Tawas library," Eleanor said as she strode back into the room.

Millicent brushed an invisible fleck of dust off her shoulder. "Well, that sure is not what I wanted to hear. Surely, there must be someone who can tell us about the '30s in the Tawas area."

"I'm afraid we're all just not that old," Eleanor said. "I was born in '32 like your grandfather."

I led the way into the kitchen where Millicent searched for pans to brown the ground beef she had brought.

"No tuna casserole?" I asked.

Millicent laughed. "Oh, I would have thought that you would have gotten sick of that by now, but if not, I can go back out to Neiman's Family Market."

"Don't be silly. What are you cooking?"

"I figured to make up a batch of chili and corn muffins."

"Sounds good. Perhaps if we feed the cleaners, they'll work harder. I can't seem to get those men to work."

Millicent added spices she found on the spice rack to the meat. "I'd be happy to give it a try. We'll have to all pitch in if we hope to have the mansion ready on Halloween."

I grumbled. "Oh, I know. Sara asked us to carve pumpkins, too. There's no way we'll be done in time. Eleanor and I have been trying to solve another case, too."

"Not to worry. Let me handle the cleaners and the pumpkin carving. You and Eleanor need to find out who killed that woman before opening day."

No pressure there. "I'm not sure I can do that. Why, we only have one more full day to do that."

"It's about five now. Perhaps you should assemble your local seniors. I'm sure somebody might have some answers."

"Actually, I had planned to, but perhaps I can ask them to come here instead of leaving. I'd hate for Sara to find us gone again."

Eleanor got on the horn and made the necessary calls, and it wasn't all that long afterward that there was a rap at the door. By now, the smell of chili wafted into the drawing room when Eleanor opened the door. Elsie Bradford strutted in, very much the peacock as she pranced about, waiting for us to say something about her latest ensemble, a powder blue pantsuit like she always wore that matched her eyes. She was the social icon of the Tawas area.

"Wow, did you get a new outfit?" Eleanor said, to which Elsie blushed.

"Why, yes, Eleanor. I have this lovely online store I like to shop at."

Next through the door were Dorothy and Frank Alton, who were already in a fight. "I told you, Frank, Eleanor wasn't the one murdered."

"Murdered?" Eleanor gasped. "Why on earth would you think that?"

"Well, we heard a woman was found dead at the Butler Mansion, and I knew you girls were here. I guess I got the wrong idea."

"I guess so," Eleanor said. "I hope you haven't come here to murder me yourself."

Dorothy fanned her face with a hand that had razor-sharp nails painted fire engine red, the jewels from her many rings sparkling. "Oh, course not, Eleanor. I thought we buried the hatchet long ago."

I personally was still waiting for the hatchet to be buried for sure. Eleanor and Dorothy had been getting along much better these days, but one just never knew for how long the peace would last. I suppose just as long as Eleanor didn't flirt with Dorothy's husband, it might be okay. Frank Alton was almost completely bald and wore a hearing aid that was almost always turned down from the way he acted when Dorothy spoke to him. They had been married for over fifty years, and if it took turning down a hearing aid to stay married, it was all for the best.

Eleanor bit her lip, answering the door once again to let in Bill and Marjory Hays, who were dressed alike, as always. Today, they were in lime green pants with matching golf shirts. It was no secret where they spent most of their time. With the current crowd, I had hoped to get through the late afternoon without discussing their recent medical diagnoses.

I led the way into the dining room where we all sat around a quite large oval table.

Caroline floated down from the ceiling, looking curiously at the newcomers.

Elsie rubbed her arms. "It's sure cool in here." When she could see her breath lingering in the air after she spoke, she added, "Of course, the place *might* be haunted."

"It's a good thing we brought the candles," Marjory said.

"Whatever for?" I asked.

"For the séance, silly."

I shook my head sharply. "We're not having one of those. Why on earth would you suggest something like that, Marjory? Since when have you been into that sort of thing?"

"I just love paranormal shows, don't you?"

"Most of those shows are fakes. Oh, someone just touched me," I mocked. "Ghosts just aren't real." I ignored Caroline who had her arms crossed.

"Well." Marjory placed her hands palm down on the table. "You don't have to burst our bubble so quickly. You had to have seen that puff of mist come from Elsie's lips. This place has to be haunted. How else can you explain that?"

I took a glass of lemonade that Millicent brought into the room. Elsie promptly removed a flask from her purse, adding some of the liquid concealed inside and passing it around the table for the others to also use.

"So is that why you're all here, then?"

They all bobbed their heads in unison.

"See, Agnes? They all believe in ghosts. How come you don't?" Eleanor asked.

"Ghosts aren't real," I insisted.

Caroline formed into a mist and disappeared beneath the table. The next thing that happened was the table started rattling and rocking like an earthquake was happening. Chairs flew back and seniors cowered together. "Stop it now, Caroline. This isn't funny."

"Who is Caroline?" Eleanor asked.

"What? I-I meant—Oh darn it. I've gone and done it again, haven't I?"

"Done what?" Elsie asked.

"Well, ever since Agnes' accident she has been acting a mite strange."

"I just think out loud, is all."

Eleanor lifted her chin and grabbed my arm, pulling me into the kitchen. "What's going on, Aggie? You're hiding something and it's time you just spit it out."

"I have nothing to say."

"Caroline was the name you were asking about earlier. Who is she?"

"I don't know. Perhaps it's the name of the ghost we followed up the stairs the other day."

"Possibly, but how did you come up with the name? I don't recall anyone mentioning any ghost by the name of Caroline associated with this mansion, but something peculiar is happening here. Did you see that table rock? I about had a heart attack on the spot."

"Me, too, but I'm not interested in hunting ghosts tonight. I'm more interested in finding out if any of the others were scammed by Katherine before she died."

"Good point, Agnes, but how are we going to get them to talk when now the only thing on their minds will be ghost hunting?"

"Leave it to me," I said as I strode back into the dining room where Elsie had a crucifix in her capable hands with the Alton's and the Hays' all behind her. "Still want to have a séance?" I asked with a smirk.

Duchess was frozen in the corner of the room, her eyes glued on the ceiling. "What is up there, girl?" I asked her. I even stared at the ceiling, but there wasn't anything there.

"Perhaps we should journey into the other room," Elsie suggested. "This room is so drafty."

I waited patiently while the others left the room and motioned for Caroline to stay like I had some kind of control over her. She was laughing so hard she flew through the wall, rattling the picture frames that were hanging there.

Of all the luck, I had a ghost attached to me who was also a comedian. That's the last thing I needed. I really needed to speak to her in private about her behavior. Today's antics did nothing to further our investigation.

I waltzed out toward the drawing room, but stopped when I spied Millicent and the cleaner in the wheelchair conversing. "You're so funny, Robert."

When I raised my brow, Millicent gave me a wink and continued to speak with Robert. I wasn't sure what she was talking about, but I had hoped it was to encourage the cleaners to work harder, although Robert didn't do all that much. But, he did clean the walls within his reach, and the floorboards.

Nobody was in the drawing room when I finally made it there, but I heard hushed voices not far off. I walked up the darkened hallway. That was a bit unsettling since I knew this house had many secrets, and I couldn't help but think there was far more that we were yet to discover.

I stumbled for a moment and landed shoulder first into the wall, but instead of the impact I expected, the wall gave way and I ended up inside a hidden corridor. It was pitch black inside, but when I felt for the way out, all I felt was a solid wall. I shivered slightly when I felt a cold draft make its way toward me. Now, not only was I trapped, but something or someone else might just be in here with me—like a spirit.

Stop it, Agnes. This is your vivid imagination having its way with you. But I wasn't able to convince myself otherwise, so I felt for my iPhone. Once I had it in my hand, I flicked on the flashlight tool, and shone it down the corridor. All that greeted me was debris and a brick wall on either side. I made my way in a hurry when I heard a rustling behind me. I feared that it was a rat or something worse. Ghosts weren't nearly as frightening as people were. Eleanor and I already knew that a corridor led from the Butler's cemetery on the hill. I wished we had inspected it more that day. It really needed to be closed up and locked in some way. If not, anyone could access the mansion without anyone knowing.

Voices carried over to where I was and I quickened my pace in their direction. Instead of pounding on the wall, I listened when I heard Elsie's voice.

"So you think Agnes has gone mad, then?" Elsie asked.

"I never said that, but she's been talking to herself—like entire conversations. I'm very worried about her."

"Have you questioned her about it?"

"Yes, and she keeps telling me that she's thinking out loud. I just think she might have rattled her head more than the doctors have said. They said she was fine, just a concussion."

"I had a friend who had an accident once," Marjory began. "After her concussion, she went into full-blown dementia."

I bit a fist. Dementia my patootie How dare these girls assume I was off my rocker?

"I-I'm not sure what's going on, but I don't think that's it. She's been fine in every other way. I just wish she'd open up to me. We've

84

been friends for a long time and this is the first time I've felt shut out."

Elsie patted Eleanor's hand. "Don't worry, old girl. Things will work out, I'm sure, but perhaps it's not all her fault. I daresay this mansion is haunted. Is it possible she's been possessed?"

"Like by a demon?"

"Yes," Marjory said. "Demonic possession is on the rise."

Eleanor snorted out a laugh. "Where, besides in some horror movie?"

"I often thought my sister Mildred was possessed before she died," Elsie said.

"Didn't you say she was bi-polar?" Eleanor asked.

"Well, yes."

"Enough of the Agnes bashing. I'm sure she's neither possessed, nor has she lost her mind. I just need to get to the bottom of what's really happening."

I searched the wall for something, anything that might help me get out of this corridor. There was whoosh of air behind me. Caroline appeared and led me down to where there was a metal lever on the wall. I pulled it down and the wall opened up for me. I raced through the opening before it closed up, panting. It took me a few minutes to regain my composure before I made my way toward the library. I walked right through Caroline who was waving her hands frantically to stop me from going inside. Nope. I wasn't about to let anything stop me from speaking my mind, although it did occur to me that perhaps I shouldn't let them know I had overheard their entire conversation.

I sprang into the room, and all eyes were on me, looking at me peculiarly, or so I thought.

"What happened to you?" Eleanor asked, a look of concern overtaking her face.

"Whatever do you mean, Eleanor? I'm just fine."

Elsie and Marjory's faces turned down into noticeable frowns, like you might see when someone wanted to tell you something but didn't. I didn't take a cue from that, though.

"Maybe you outta take a look in the mirror," Bill suggested. "You look like you were stuck in a broom closet."

"Bill," Marjory scolded. "That's not very nice. I'm sure Agnes has a good explanation about her whereabouts and why she's covered in cob webs."

I raced over to a mirror that hung on the opposite wall and took in my appearance. Eleanor rushed over and began pulling off the cobwebs as I brushed dust from my clothing the best that I could. "Oh, wow. I never expected to get that dirty. I assure you, it's quite explainable—" I clammed up then because I didn't want to tell them the truth. I'd rather have a discussion with Eleanor about the matter later. I wasn't sure it's common knowledge about all the hidden passageways in the mansion, so for now I'd keep that to myself. I really wanted to tell Eleanor about the ghost, but I just was so unsure how she'd take it. I even wondered if she'd believe me at all.

"I-I ..." Eleanor's eyes narrowed slightly as I added, "I must have brushed against one of the walls. There are still plenty of cobwebs in this place."

"Yes, like inside your rattled head," Eleanor said in a whisper as she passed me on her way from the library.

I shrugged and left the room to catch up with Eleanor. "Wait up, Eleanor. I have something to tell you."

Eleanor turned in a huff. "I'm done with your wild tales. It's obvious that you'd rather not tell me what's *really* going on."

Before I could say anything, Eleanor made her way toward the drawing room. I took my leave and cleaned myself up before I returned. Mr. Wilson was engaged in a discussion about trout fishing with Frank Alton, who nodded like he heard every word he had said when I returned.

The room had a white fireplace and mantle and not a thing gothic looking in the room. Leather sofas and chairs were arranged around the room with a large-screen television affixed to one of the walls. Dorothy Alton clicked through the channels until she came to the news, settling herself back on the loveseat next to her beloved Frank.

The news reporter made an announcement about the woman's body found at the Butler Mansion, identifying her as Katherine Clark. According to the reporter, the police had no current leads in the case and were asking the public for tips.

"Well, that's just awful," Bernice said as she pulled a pipe from her pocket.

"Bernice, you'll have to take that smoke outside. There's no smoking in the Butler Mansion."

Bernice wet her lips with her thick tongue and shot back with, "Since when do you abide by rules, Agnes? It wasn't all that long ago that you were butting heads with Sheriff Peterson about your investigations. Eleanor mentioned that you two found that Katherine's body."

"It's true, but I get along much better with Peterson these days."

"We found her body," Eleanor said. "Did any of you know her?"

I searched the group for any sign that they had, in fact, known the woman, but everyone had blank expressions on their faces, other than Elsie who had her eyes fixated on a yellow vase on the end table.

"How about you, Elsie?" I asked.

She locked eyes with me then and said, "I'd rather discuss this with you and Eleanor privately."

"I understand, but have any of you ever been approached by anyone asking you to invest in a solar energy company?"

"Sure have," Mr. Wilson said. "But it weren't no lady, that's for sure."

"Meaning what?" Eleanor asked.

"Just that it was some floozy I met at Barnacle Bill's." When Eleanor's face reddened, he added, "I was there for Mexican Monday. They have the best wet burritos in town."

"Go on, Wilson," I encouraged him.

"She was dressed in a red dress and was damn near spilling out of it. I don't remember much about the company she wanted me to invest in. When I told her I wasn't looking for investments at my age, she disappeared real quick like, which was just as well since my food had arrived."

"Did you notice where she went?"

"Nope. I was starving."

"Do you know what Katherine Clark looks like?"

"I can't say I do. That name doesn't sound familiar to me."

I had no clue what I would do now since I didn't have any pictures of Katherine.

"There was some strumpet after my Frank the other day at the pier, but she ran off when I threatened to feed her a mouthful of knuckles." Dorothy paused for a moment, and continued, "Now that Wilson mentioned it, she wore a red dress, too."

"It's awfully embarrassing to admit you were swindled," Elsie said. "I'm a very proud woman, but since some of you have been so candid, I have to admit that a woman in a red dress gave me a stock tip about a solar company, International Energy, I think she called it. She told me I could get in on the ground floor. I don't know why, but I gave her the money. She sounded so convincing and the forms I filled out looked official."

"Did you check up on them first, like online, or have an attorney look over the documents?"

Elsie hung her head. "No, Katherine told me time was of the essence. So I went to the bank and withdrew the funds."

"Why not write a check?"

"She wanted cash. They put a hold on substantial checks. You know that, Agnes."

88

I squeezed Elsie's shoulder. "It's not your fault, Elsie. We senior citizens make for perfect victims. It makes me sick that someone would be taken in like that. How much did you give her?"

"Twenty thousand."

Frank Alton whistled. "Wow, Elsie. You've never been one to let your cash stray far from you."

She squared her shoulders. "No need to rub it in, Frank."

"Don't blame my Frank just because you made a bad decision. I sure hope you won't lose your house," huffed Dorothy.

Elsie sat down in a huff. "I'm not that stupid, Dorothy."

"Well, you sure were stupid enough not to at least check out the woman. You could at least have checked on Facebook."

"Oh, are you on Facebook, Dorothy?" I asked.

"Yes, but I'm only on there to keep track of my family. That granddaughter of mine has been dating one of the Hill boys on and off. I can't tell you how upset that makes me."

I imagined she might feel that way since the Hill boys are part of the Michigan Militia, but there's no sense fussing about anyone your grown-up granddaughter decides to date. I should know, since my granddaughter, Sophia, dated Trooper Sales before she ended up pregnant. But, he made it right and married her before the baby was born. Besides, Curt and Curtis Hill weren't all that bad. They'd helped me out on occasions like when my awning came crashing down after Eleanor had crashed into it once.

"No need to make Elsie feel bad. She wasn't the only one in town to be conned out of money," I said without elaborating further.

"Nope," Eleanor said. "Even Jack Winston got conned."

Gasps split the air. "Well," Elsie said. She quickly diverted her eyes. "That's—"

"Well, deserved," Dorothy butted in. "The way that man carries on with all those bimbos is just dreadful. Why, back when his wife was alive, he even cheated on her."

Elsie cleared her throat, staggering to her feet. "I really could use a glass of cold water. I'm parched."

Eleanor went in search of the water and returned, handing her the glass. "Now, Dorothy, no need to wish ill of anyone. Jack's life isn't—"

"He's not deserving of getting conned any more that Elsie was," I interjected, giving Eleanor a nudge in the ribs. "No need to share all of Jack's secrets," I whispered to Eleanor.

"Sorry, Agnes. I didn't think."

That is classic Eleanor. She's never one who thinks before she speaks, and doles out more information than is necessary. It's none of anyone's concern that Jack has been paying money out for his female companionship.

"Elsie, would you mind speaking with us in private?"

"That's just as well," Bernice said. "I have to take my cats home—if I can find all of them."

Bill and Marjory Hays made their way to the door, following Bernice out.

"I don't see why we have to leave," Dorothy said.

"Because they don't want you in their business is why," Frank blubbered.

"But I'm Elsie's friend. I'm sure she won't mind me staying."

"Confound it, woman, we're leaving, now!" Frank made way for the door, muttering something about him wishing he had listened to his mother and stayed single.

Dorothy trailed after him. "Oh, Frank."

Once the door slammed shut and cars rumbled out of the drive, Mr. Wilson struggled to get off the chair. Eleanor rushed over and helped him get up. He said, "I'll busy myself elsewhere. I haven't seen my granddaughter since we arrived."

CHAPTER NINE

When we were alone, Elsie said, "Maybe we should go to the library. That way, nobody can overhear our conversation."
Thinking about how I heard plenty from the hidden passageway, I doubted it was completely safe, but since I hadn't seen any signs that anyone else had been in there, I figured it was as good a place as anywhere.

We strode to the library and it was eerily silent. Outside, the sky had already begun to darken and all I could think about was how Eleanor and I had to stay the night in this haunted mansion.

In the library, there was a desk that was next to a window that overlooked the spacious lawn and rose gardens. Dark shapes were visible for a moment, but they took on the shape of the cleaners that Sara had hired, minus the one in the wheelchair who I presumed was still talking to Mr. Wilson's granddaughter. I reminded myself to speak with her later about what she was up to; hoping that it only had to do with getting the cleaners to work faster.

Eleanor sank into a leather chair near the desk, with Elsie taking the other one. I sat behind the desk and interlaced my fingers. "How did you *really* find out about the business opportunity?"

Elsie blinked a few times and said, "What do you mean, *really*?"

"I couldn't help but notice how you reacted when I told everyone Jack Winston had also been swindled."

"You mean when *I* told them, Agnes," Eleanor said.

"Oh, bother. Does it really matter who told whom what, El?"

"Well, it does when you don't give me credit for my part in this investigative business."

"I give you plenty of credit, El. Jeez, can we just question Elsie, already?"

"Yes," Eleanor began. "Why did you react like that when I said Jack's name? It's almost like it wasn't a surprise to you."

"So you already knew about Jack?" I added.

Elsie's face flushed. "Yes, Jack kinda gave me the tip, and I went all the way to Bay Port to meet with Katherine. It was then that she told me she had planned to come to East Tawas, but she needed the cash right away or I'd miss out on the deal. That time was of the essence. She insisted on cash, you see."

"Why would Jack Winston even tell you about this tip?" I asked, perplexed. *Unless he was part of the scam*, was my thought.

"Well, I've known Jack for years. We bumped into each other at the library. I didn't even know he was staying with his son. Word had it that he had lost his house. He told me about how his son was limiting his funds and he found a way to make back all the money he had lost. All he had to do was invest money short term."

"Did you ask him how he planned to get the money from his son?"

"I told him to look around for a checkbook. I was quite sure his son didn't keep it under lock and key."

"Well, it seems like he should have. Why take Jack's word for it, though?" I pressed.

Elsie sighed. "Jack and I go way back."

"Is there any truth that you and Jack had an affair years ago?"

"That's none of our business, Agnes Barton!" Eleanor shouted.

"I'm trying to establish a connection between Elsie and Jack. Why else would he tell her about the business opportunity?"

"I have nothing to hide now, but I swear I'm so sorry for all of that. His wife was one of my friends, but I called it off real quick-like, before things had gotten too out of hand," Elsie explained. "I swear that I never meant to hurt anyone."

"That's all in the past, Elsie," I said. "What I'd like to know is what happened lately. So, Jack was just giving you a tip for old time's sake?"

"Well, I think the man is a little sweet on me after all these years. He told me none of those younger women holds a candle next to me."

"So Katherine turned up in town and then what?"

"I had agreed to introduce her to my friends, but then Jack told me that the company, International Energy, had gone belly-up. That all of his money, probably all our money, was long gone. He tried to call Katherine. I tried to call Katherine, but she wouldn't return our calls. When Jack did find her, she threatened to turn him into the police if he didn't quit bothering her."

"Did you report what happened to the police?"

Elsie's shoulders slumped. "I was too ashamed to admit we had been taken."

"Too ashamed?" Eleanor said. "What about all the other potential victims she hadn't scammed yet? I can't believe you didn't call the police."

"Well, both Jack and I had turned over the cash to her in Huron County, not Iosco. I didn't think Sheriff Peterson would be able to do anything about it."

"Other than put the word out, at least," Eleanor said, her arms folded across her chest.

"Now, Eleanor. There's no need to be so cross with Elsie. It's hard to admit that you've been taken by a con artist."

"Jack felt so bad and promised to make it right."

My brow shot up. "Oh, and did he say how?"

"No, but he was very angry. You wouldn't like Jack when he's angry."

I recalled a few times when he did get angry, and he was quite scary, but one time Eleanor didn't back down a bit and he got entangled in a lawn chair, of all things. Luckily, for Eleanor and me, we were able to flee the scene before he had freed himself. I personally wouldn't give two cents for Jack. I had managed to see him in a different light, but now wondered if it was the right light.

"He must have said something more," Eleanor said. "Please, every little bit might help."

"Jack told me he found out that Katherine took a job at the Butler Mansion and we both figured it was a cover for her con business. He told me he'd catch her unaware at the mansion and get us our money back, or—"

"Or what?" Eleanor interjected. "Did he say he'd harm the woman?"

"I-I shouldn't say. I mean, I don't want to get Jack into any trouble."

"You'll both be in trouble if you don't spill the beans, and quick," Eleanor said. "I have half a mind to call in the sheriff right now."

"Eleanor!" I shouted.

"Or else. Jack said he'd get our money back or else. I wasn't sure what he meant."

"Did you ask him what he meant?" I asked, as the ghost floated through the ceiling.

"No, I didn't."

"You didn't care is why," Eleanor went on to say. "You should have called the police and had ample opportunity to do so, and now Katherine is dead, leaving both you and Jack on the suspect list."

Elsie sprung to her feet. "But I didn't do anything. I swear I didn't."

"How much were you in for, *really*?" I asked, giving Eleanor a dirty look. I couldn't believe how hostile she was acting towards Elsie. I had an idea it was far more than the twenty thousand she told us she handed over when the others were here.

Elsie pursed her lips and finally said, "Fifty thousand."

I bit a fist, Eleanor flopped back on her chair, her arms thrown back and the ghost smacked her head on the wall, whatever that was all about.

"Now that's a lot of greenbacks," Eleanor said. "I'm sorry I was so hard on you. I just—well—I thought there might even be more victims other than you and Jack."

"I don't blame you. I blame myself for listening to Jack to begin with. In the beginning, I even blamed him for being part of the scam."

"What did he have to say to that?" I asked.

"He denied it, of course, but I can't get that doubt out of my mind completely. Then when he told me he'd get our money back, I just knew he couldn't be a part of it. He was so enraged."

"I had hoped to keep this under wraps, but I really think we need to pull Sheriff Peterson in on this one."

"Oh, please don't do that. Can't you just investigate the case yourself?"

"Yes, we can and will, but if I don't tell Peterson, he won't be happy. Besides, he might just share some information with us, too. I can't help but wonder who this Katherine really is, and why she'd stay in town after scamming the two of you."

"Beats me, Agnes, but I swear I'm not in cahoots with Jack Winston. I was angry, but not enough to murder someone."

"So you admit that Jack seemed angry enough to murder Katherine?"

Elsie threw up her arms. "Now don't be putting words in my mouth. I never said that. Sure, Jack was mad as a wet hen, but murder? Now that's a stretch." Elsie glanced at her watch. "Are you two through interrogating me now? It's almost time for my night time pills."

"This wasn't an interrogation, Elsie. For the life of me, I don't know how to proceed. Jack was our only lead. I can't help but wonder why Katherine would come to the area if she'd swindled you two, is all. How could she be sure you wouldn't go to the police?"

"Well," Eleanor said. "If they both paid the woman in cash, there'd be no paper trail. It would be their word against Katherine's."

"But Elsie and Jack are ... er—"

"Upstanding citizens for the most part, or at least Elsie is. Jack Winston's reputation stands for itself, not that he's ever broken any laws other than using medicinal locally grown products without the proper prescription,"

"From my recollection," Elsie said, "Jack wasn't the only one in town doing that. You both—"

I interjected. "Oh, no, you don't. Neither El nor I have ever smoked any of that wacky weed that Rose Lee used to grow. Besides, she's gone out of that business and is now growing plants for her potpourri."

"All I'm saying is, don't be too quick to nail this on Jack. We can't be the only two people who that woman has conned, and that's all I have to say on the subject."

I gave up talking about this, too. Eleanor and I led Elsie to the door and she tore out of the drive with a scattering of dust and stones.

"Well, are we really going to do it, Agnes? Tell Sheriff Peterson what we've found out? He'll be mad that we haven't brought him in sooner."

"Not as much as if we never told him what's going on."

"So just to be clear, what are we planning to tell him?"

I thought for a moment. "Not sure, but perhaps we should keep that secret passageway to ourselves for now."

"Good point, but what about the vanishing suitcase?"

"Leave it to me, El. Just follow my lead when we get to the sheriff's department."

"The sheriff won't be there this time of night. We'll have to call him at home."

I shook my head. "Do you really expect me to call Clem at home?"

"Doesn't seem like we have much of a choice, but you'd better hurry. It's six o'clock. We only have one more solid day of investigating. Tomorrow is Halloween. We'll have to be back here at the mansion by seven o'clock when this mansion will be open to the public."

That bothered me. How were gonna ever be able to solve this case in time, and what about Caroline? I have yet to figure out who she is and how she's connected to this mansion. After Eleanor goes to bed, I'm going to have a talk with my new partner, the ghost, Caroline. I was so torn, but I just was not ready to tell Eleanor about her, I still haven't come to terms with her myself, nor the seeing and speaking to the ghost part.

Chapter Ten

Eleanor and I argued about which one of us was going to call the sheriff, and Millicent finally made the call. Eleanor and I were parked in the dining room, enjoying a bowl of chili that Millicent had made along with her special corn muffins.

Millicent introduced us to the cleaners, Larry and Gary, who shook our hands, apologizing for their behavior earlier in the day. Robert, who was the one confined to a wheelchair, appeared to be in a little better spirits since he had spent time in Millicent's company. Eleanor and I had welcomed them to eat with us, but they insisted they had to leave by dark. Of course, it was already dark, but I almost wondered by the wary looks they exchanged with each other if they were afraid of something, like this mansion, for one. They did promise to be back at first light and finish up. From the looks of the downstairs, they had done a good job. At first, I had my reservations, but even I had to admit that I was prone to be wrong sometimes.

After the men left, I had to ask Millicent, "What's your secret with getting those men to work harder?"

"I didn't really do anything much at all, just talked to them a little bit. They really aren't all that bad when you get talking to them. They're quite the fishermen from the way they talk. I'm meeting them at five to go fishing tomorrow."

"Like, five in the morning?" Eleanor asked with a laugh.

"Sure. From the way they talk, the fish get up early around these parts."

"And how do you feel about staying here in town? Don't you live in Saginaw?"

"Yes. But, there's nothing back in Saginaw for me. Gramps needs me."

Mr. Wilson slammed his cup on the table. "Nonsense. I'm fine as a fiddle, but I must admit it's been so nice having you around. You remind me of my late wife," he sniveled for a moment, batting at the invisible tears. "I sure miss my old girl."

Eleanor darted from the room, returning with a peach cobbler that Millicent also made. Before the ice cream had a chance to melt on the cobbler, Sheriff Peterson walked through the door. His hat wasn't on and his hair had been slicked back. It wasn't an effort to look neat or well-kept. He sweated profusely normally.

I noticed the sheriff didn't appear to be upset we'd interrupted his dinner, and I offered him a bowl of cobbler for his trouble of coming all the way here.

"Thanks, don't mind if I do. I have a weakness for sweets. The wife won't allow me to eat sweets at home."

I understood what he meant. That's what wives of unfit men would do, and lord knows, his wife was justified enough to limit his sugar intake.

He put a spoonful of the cobbler in his mouth, his face lighting up in pleasure. "This tastes great."

"Thanks," Millicent gushed. "It's my grandma's recipe."

Mr. Wilson rose to his full height and made some excuse about leaving us to handle our business with Millicent in tow, who gave us a quick wink before she left the room.

Peterson wiped his mouth with a napkin and asked, "I'm sure you didn't call me out to give me dessert, so what gives?"

"Actually, we have uncovered some information that might be pertinent to your investigation."

His brow furrowed. "I see. And you're actually sharing it? I'm impressed, Agnes. How unexpected of you. I might even be inclined to share a few details with you, too."

I about fell off my chair. "Really? That sure would be great."

"Like what kind of information, Peterson?" asked Eleanor suspiciously. "Isn't that against police policy?"

"Yes. I don't want you wasting your time chasing ghosts, so to speak, but I expect you to keep this between us."

Caroline floated into the chair next to Peterson at the mention of ghosts.

Eleanor tapped my foot with hers, and whispered, "I can't believe this." Turning to the sheriff and smiling, she said, "So what's the information you're sharing?"

Totally dismissing Eleanor, Peterson said, "You first, Agnes."

Eleanor leaned back in her chair in a huff. "Go ahead, Agnes. Obviously, I'm not important."

I gave Eleanor a look. "Oh, stop, would you? I'm sure the sheriff didn't mean anything by that."

He cleared his throat. "As you were about to say?"

"Eleanor and I have searched the mansion. Sara Knoxville, the actress, asked us to oversee the preparations of the opening of the bed and breakfast. Anyway, we found a suitcase with some letters in it."

Peterson leaned forward. "Haven't we gone through this already? Has the suitcase suddenly reappeared?"

Without answering his question, I continued, "Well, we did find a suitcase with clothing in it, and these letters." I searched my purse, like through every compartment. "Gee, that's strange. I was certain I had the letters in here."

"What letters?"

"It was mail sent to Katherine Clark from Jack Winston. He was sending her letters asking to see her in person about a personal matter they needed to clear up."

"So you had mail that you found linking someone to our victim and you didn't think that it was important enough to turn over to me sooner, and now you've lost the evidence?"

"I wanted to question Jack first. I really can't imagine where the letters are now, or how I could have lost them."

Peterson stood up. "Show me where you found the suitcase again. I want to see for sure that there's nothing hidden there that you don't want me to know about."

Caroline bobbed ahead of Peterson on the stairs. I strolled to the room where we found the suitcase and all of the windows were wide open, a swift breeze blowing in. Eleanor dashed over to close the windows, but grunted in frustration. The sheriff gave her hand, easily closing the window.

I opened the closet and, lo and behold, the suitcase was there. He pulled gloves out of his pocked and pulled it out, setting it in on the bed. When he opened the suitcase, a musky smell was present like it hadn't been opened in decades. All of the clothing was folded neatly inside, too. He carefully pulled out an article of clothing and shook it open. It was a floral cape dress.

"That looks vintage," Eleanor exclaimed.

"Yes, like something someone from the 30s might wear."

Peterson then pulled out picture frames that were in the bottom of the suitcase. They were black and whites, depicting a woman in her thirties dressed in a variety of fancy dresses of the1930s.

When I spotted one of a man, I asked Peterson, "Can I see that one closer?"

"Nope, it's evidence."

"How is that evidence? The contents look like they have been in the back of that suitcase since the 30s. There's nothing in there that looks like it belongs to Katherine."

"It can't rule it out, either."

"But that belongs to Sara Knoxville. You just can't remove what could be the belongings of her ancestors."

Peterson fell silent. "I'm confiscating them until a thorough analysis can be done down at the station. I'll turn them over to Sara if we find that it's not pertinent to the investigation."

I grumbled and followed Peterson down the stairs and he turned and asked me, "So what did you turn up when you questioned Jack Winston?"

"He told us that Katherine Clark had convinced him to invest money into a solar energy company."

Peterson set the suitcase on a table and took out a notebook. "I'm listening."

"International Energy," I said. "It seems that even Elsie Bradford was taken in by the scheme."

"Yes, Jack told Elsie about the business opportunity," Eleanor added. "But apparently Jack figured out too late that they were scammed."

"If this is true, why didn't either of them call the police?"

"Beats me," Eleanor said. "I almost wondered if Jack was part of the scam. He did seem awfully upset when we told him Katherine had been murdered."

"And how did you come to the conclusion that Katherine had been murdered when an autopsy hadn't even been performed yet?"

"Well, I-I—" I struggled for words. "Is that what you were going to tell us, Peterson, that Katherine was murdered?"

"Actually, no. What I had planned to tell you was to keep this case to yourselves. The woman who died in this mansion is not Katherine Clark. At this point, we don't want to let on that the woman who died here had used an alias, and now I think I know why. If she had scammed Jack and Elsie, why did she stay in town?"

"So what is her real name?"

"We don't know as of yet. That's why I need every shred of evidence I can get to figure out who she really is. Her body has yet to be picked up from the coroner, either, which has me wondering, but when it is, we're going to be ready. The coroner has promised to call us immediately when and if someone shows up to claim the body."

"We've wondered ourselves about why she'd stay in town after taking those two for a ride, but it would be their word against hers. They paid her in cash. Elsie said she filled out paperwork, but didn't say if she had a copy of it."

"I'll check that out. Thanks."

"Both Elsie and Jack have told us the same details. Frank Alton said a woman in a red dress approached him. I didn't have any pictures of Katherine to verify it, though," Eleanor said.

He jotted down a few more notes. "Anything else?"

I wanted to ask him about the couple who tried to kidnap my son and me, but I didn't want to mess in Stuart's investigation, whatever it entailed. I vowed to find out what Stuart was really up to, but I was too busy with other things.

Before Peterson had gotten to the suitcase, it fell to the floor with a clunk, dumping the contents onto the floor. I spied an oval picture frame and kicked it beneath a chair and out of sight. Peterson knelt, packed the suitcase and left, telling us to call him if we found out anything else.

"How did that suitcase fall on the floor like that?" Eleanor asked.

I didn't see a trace that Caroline was in the room when I responded with, "I don't know, but there sure are some peculiar things happening at the mansion."

"That goes without saying, and boy, am I bushed. I'm heading to bed."

Mr. Wilson and Millicent appeared through the French doors and announced they'd be leaving, promising to bring Halloween decorations tomorrow.

"Are you sure you don't want to stay?" I asked them.

Mr. Wilson's face paled a bit, quite a feat since he had a gray pallor most of the time. "Just be sure to keep my Eleanor safe tonight.

I'm not sure why either of you would want to be staying the night in a haunted mansion, but you're welcome to it."

"And what have you seen that makes you think that it's haunted?"

"Besides that man upstairs, nothing."

"Wh-What man?"

Millicent shrugged. "When we were outside, we saw a man through the third floor window. He was transparent." She bit a nail. "Please, don't stay here. It's not safe."

"It's just as safe as anywhere else, and even if this place is haunted, ghosts can't hurt you."

"No, but they can scare you to death," Mr. Wilson said with a curt nod.

I escorted them to their car so I could take a look at the mansion from outside. After Millicent tore out of the drive, I examined every window, but I didn't see any ghosts. Not even Caroline. Where was she, anyway? Was she responsible for pushing over that suitcase? I had more questions than that, but unless I saw her when I went inside, they would have to wait until I saw Caroline again.

I strolled back inside, being sure to lock all of the doors. I quickly changed into my nightgown and climbed into bed. There was a bathroom connected to the bedroom and I left a light on in there so I wouldn't be in complete darkness.

I snapped my eyelids shut, trying not to think about ghosts and haunted mansions, but that was so hard to do when you're sleeping in one. I concentrated on my breathing and managed to fall asleep. I about jumped out of my skin as a clock chimed—three from the first floor, I thought—but it was so loud it vibrated me right out of bed. I could still hear the vibrations and struggled to Eleanor's room, but she was fast asleep. There was light at the end of the hallway, and when I realized it was in the same room that we had found the suitcase, I cautiously made my way there.

I walked inside and found Caroline on the bed, humming to herself. She glanced up at me, but kept on humming. The closet was open and full of clothing, all from the 30s. On the floor were shoes neatly arranged from the same period—many of the heeled Oxford shoes with suede soles.

"Suede soles?" I asked Caroline.

She stopped her humming. "Of course. They're perfect for dancing," she gushed. "I went dancing every weekend, and had me plenty of fellas to dote on me."

"So what brought you here to the Tawas area?"

"Oh, well, I met me a dashing man." She got up off the bed and began making dancing movements. "I just love to swing dance, don't you?"

"I can't say that I've ever tried. My Tom was not much of a dancer. So did you do that in the 30s?"

She swirled her skirt that was about as transparent as she was. "Oh, yes,"

"But the 30s were during the Great Depression."

"Yes, but in the circles I ran, believe me, it wasn't a problem."

It was on the tip of my tongue to ask her to elaborate, but just then, Eleanor entered the room. "Agnes, dear. Who on earth are you talking to?"

My mouth fell open. "I ... I." I then stared over to where Caroline was, but she disappeared in a puff of smoke that apparently Eleanor couldn't see. "The truth is—"

Eleanor crossed her arms across her ample bosom. "The truth ... I can't wait to hear this."

"The truth is, I see dead people."

Eleanor blinked repeatedly. "Come again?"

"You heard me."

"I thought I heard you, but are you even awake or are you sleep walking?"

"Well, I'm talking to you so that must mean I'm awake. Oh, bother. You've scared her away, Eleanor."

106

"Scared who away, exactly?"

"The ghost. She's suddenly shy, although she certainly wasn't earlier when she rattled the table when we had company."

Eleanor shook her head. "Maybe we should talk about this in the morning. I don't' think you're thinking clearly."

I frowned and threw my arms up into the air, making way for my room.

"Don't you dare walk away from me, Agnes."

I froze in my tracks and whirled, only to have Eleanor run headlong into me. We both ran into the wall and it opened behind us, propelling us both into a passageway. The wall closed behind us. "Oh, great. Not again!" I wailed.

"Again?" Eleanor said.

"Yes. I was in here earlier when you were all talking about me in the library." Except that we're on the second floor, not the first.

Eleanor now clung to my arm. "Oh, it wasn't all me, and for the record, I don't think you're nuts. I sure hope you don't see any dead people now."

"How can I when the lights are all out? I can't see my hand in front of my face."

"How ever are we going to get out of here?"

"Well, I'm not sure."

"Can't you call one of those dead people to help us?"

"I thought you didn't want to see any dead people."

"I don't, but if it will get us out of here, I'm game."

I gingerly touched the wall and made my way to where I thought was the way out, or as best as I could recollect. When I took a few more steps, lights turned on and we were at a staircase like the one we had climbed down the other day.

"I think this leads to the cemetery," I said.

"Cemetery?" Eleanor whined. "I don't want to be wandering around in a cemetery in the dead of night."

"How about we don't use words like *dead*."

"Fine with me, but why can't we just figure out how to get back into the room where this pathway had led the other day. You know the room we found the suitcase in?"

I took a step in that direction and the lights went out. "Oh, my. I really don't think they want us to go that way."

"They?"

"Or whoever just cut the lights on and then off."

"Well, it could be a sensor," Eleanor suggested.

"Oh, good point, El."

"So what should we do now?"

"I guess we'll have to be tromping around in that cemetery since we can't find our way to get back inside from here."

I led the way and we carefully descended the stairs, taking hold of the handrail. "I don't suppose you have a cell phone in your nightgown, Eleanor?"

"No, and you?"

"We really need to buy nightgowns with pockets," I said with a chuckle.

"At least you haven't lost your wit, Agnes."

"No, not at all, but believe me, I didn't expect for these things to happen."

"Nope, I suppose not." Eleanor pointed ahead of me. "Look, it's another door."

I made my way there and opened the door that was thankfully unlocked. I walked through with Eleanor closely behind me. It was cold and damp on the other side, and once the door closed behind us, I realized we were in the cemetery. I tried to open the door again, but it was now locked.

"Remember, there was a lever," Eleanor reminded me.

I felt for the handle, and when yanked it down, it came off in my hands. "Yup, El. There was a handle, but now I must have broken it off somehow."

Eleanor gasped. "What now?"

I stared at the full moon overhead. "We can find our way back to the mansion since the moon is so full tonight."

Eleanor took the lead this time and we strolled through the cemetery, careful not to disturb any headstones, or rouse any ghosts. So far, I was collecting ghosts like savings stamps.

We pushed the iron fence open and soon were following the road that led back to the mansion. Headlights came at us, swerving slightly before they slammed on their brakes and backed up.

The interior light came on and we were staring at Curt and Curtis Hill, Rosa Lee Hill's boys and Michigan Militia members. "What on earth?" Curtis asked from the driver's seat. "What are you two doing out here?"

"Now that's a story with no easy answer," I said. "I don't suppose you boys could give us a ride back to the Butler Mansion?"

"We sure can, but why are you staying there? Isn't that place haunted or something?"

"Or something," I agreed. "We're staying there to ready it for a Halloween opening. It's opening as a bed and breakfast."

Curt hopped in the back so that Eleanor and I could ride up front. "Where are you boys coming from?" I asked.

"Like you said, Miss Agnes, that's a question with no easy answer."

I nodded in the darkness. "I'm willing to keep your whereabouts to ourselves if you don't tell your ma about this one."

"That's a deal. Mum's the word."

Of course, I hadn't known these boys to be rule breakers since they were quite young, but it's hard to keep boys on the right path when they are teenagers. Rosa Lee Hill wasn't just their mother, but a good friend of ours, even though we hadn't seen her all that much lately.

Curtis yanked his wheel sharply and came up the driveway fast. When he slammed on his brakes, Eleanor and I about toppled over.

"I hope you have the keys, Miss Agnes."

"Actually, I was hoping you boys could get us inside."

"Yeah," Eleanor said. "Don't you know how to pick a lock?"

"Now, Eleanor."

"We sure can, but are you sure you have permission to be here? I'd rather not face the sheriff in the middle of the night."

I thought about that for a moment and said, "Yes, I'm positive. Open the door and you two can go about your business."

Curtis pulled out a small box from his back pocket and removed two metal bars. I held the box for him while he inserted the metal picks into the lock and worked them until we heard a click. I handed him back the box and waved to the Hill boys as they took their leave.

Once they left, I closed the door and Eleanor and I slumped down into chairs in the drawing room, a room I'd call the living room. "I'm sure glad those Hill boys don't ask many questions," I said.

"You got that one right. I can't help but wonder what they were doing out and about this time of night."

"Well, I suppose we don't need to be concerned about that since we have our own troubles." I half expected Eleanor to drill me about the whole 'seeing ghosts' thing, but she yawned and I suggested we go on back to bed. I had forgotten all about the picture frame I had kicked under a chair and I retrieved it before retiring upstairs to our respective rooms. I slid the frame into a drawer and snuggled into bed, falling fast asleep within minutes.

CHAPTER ELEVEN

After I woke up and showered, I donned a pair of gray slacks with a short-sleeved sweater with a high neckline that zipped up in the back. As I slipped my feet into flats, Eleanor rushed through the door, her face bright and cheerful.

I surveyed Eleanor's clothing with raised brow. She wore denim pants and a black t-shirt with a huge goofy faced jack-o'-lantern in the center.

"Looks like you're ready for Halloween, Eleanor."

"Yes, and it looks like you're not."

"Yes, well, we do have more investigating to do. I had planned to pay the coroner a visit. I wonder if we can weasel out of him the cause of Katherine's death."

"Doubtful, but we can give it a shot. Maybe we should pick up Martha first. She's good at swaying men."

"True, but the coroner won't just hand out information like that. There are privacy issues and a police investigation."

"True, but never underestimate the power of Martha's effect on men. How else would she be able to entice so many?'

"Beats me, but you're right about that. She obviously has her talents."

Mr. Wilson and Millicent arrived right before we left, just as the cleaning guys, Gary and Larry, showed up. They pushed a wheelchair to the passenger side of their van, and Robert propelled his body from the van to the wheelchair with ease. I was quite impressed with his upper body strength. They nodded in greeting as Eleanor and I stood on the porch. Gary helped pull the wheelchair up the few steps to the porch, where they greeted Millicent with wide smiles as they entered the mansion with their cleaning supplies.

I waited until they were long gone before I asked Millicent, "So what did you find out about the microfiche? Does the library in town have any?"

"Oh, no, but as it turns out, Connie Mathews has acquired quite the collection of old newspapers. She's a history buff of sorts."

"Connie Mathews? I'm not sure I even know who she is," I said.

"She's worked at the sheriff's department in years past, but she's been retired for quite some time." Millicent handed me a slip of paper with an address in Oscoda scrawled on it.

Once we were settled in the car, Eleanor asked, "So where are we going, really?"

"Well, we could go ask Martha to pay a visit to the coroner."

"We could, but shouldn't we accompany her?"

"Could do that, but you see, I think ... err ... Martha will have better luck without us."

Eleanor folded her arms across her chest. "No fair." She choked out the words. "I wanted to go."

Well, I suppose I should go into more detail than I did last night. "You see," I began just as Caroline appeared in the back seat.

"Go ahead, Agnes," Caroline's hollowed voice split the uncomfortable silence. "Tell her all about me. I can't wait to hear this."

"Would you stop it, Caroline? I'm trying to tell her, okay?"

Eleanor's eyes widened. "Caroline? I thought you were seeing Katherine's ghost."

"Actually, no. You see, ever since my accident, a ghost has attached itself to me. Her name is Caroline."

Eleanor scratched her head. "Are you sure? Seems more likely that you'd see Katherine's ghost."

"Nope, I've been seeing Caroline. She's the one I've been talking to. At first, she wouldn't talk to me, but now she won't shut up. I don't think she knows how she died. I believe she died in the 30s."

"What makes you think that?" Eleanor asked. "Did she tell you that?"

"Not exactly, but she did scrawl on my windshield when it was all fogged up."

"I see, but is there any other reason you think she's from the 30s?"

"Caroline wears clothing from the 30s, although it looks transparent, like her."

"Just like the clothing that was in that suitcase?"

"Yes, and I strongly suspect that she is connected to the Butler Mansion in some way."

"So where are we off to?"

"I'd like to check out what this Connie has hidden in her house. If she had old newspapers, I'd sure like to go through them."

"What would they have to do with Katherine's murder?"

"Nothing as far as I know, but I think it's only fair that I find out who Caroline really is since she insists on being my traveling companion."

"I what?" Caroline huffed. "I have better things to do, you know." Her face lit up in a soft glow. "I know! I'll keep an eye on those men at the mansion. I just don't trust those cleaners."

Before I could say anything, Caroline was off in a puff of smoke.

I glanced back at Eleanor. "It doesn't have anything to do with Katherine as far as I know, but I'll check in with Martha about the coroner after we see what Connie has to say about the old newspapers."

"Why not check out the state library? I'm sure we can find microfiche files somewhere."

"Possibly, but why go to all that trouble when we might be able to locate them closer to home?"

"Fine, but I'd rather focus on one investigation, not two. I don't see how finding out who your ghost is has anything to do with Katherine's death."

"Unless, of course, Caroline's death is related to the mansion. We saw a ghost the other day, if you recall, and I've seen the ghost of a man, too; what if one of those ghosts caused Katherine's death?"

Eleanor leaned back. "Wow, this is one humdinger of a case. I can't wait to see how it turns out."

I gave Martha a quick call to ask her to see what she could get out of the coroner, Walter Smitty, reminding her to turn on the charm. As if she wouldn't, since it's sort of how Martha rolls.

"Where are we headed now?" Eleanor asked.

"Oscoda, Evergreen Avenue."

Eleanor pulled out a tube of red lipstick, amply smearing it on her lips. "Stop somewhere so I can get a pop. I'm thirsty."

I nodded in agreement since I was thirsty myself. When I made it to US 23, I drove the ten minutes it took to get from the Butler Mansion to East Tawas. We made a quick stop at the Bay Party Store. When we walked through the doors, the fragrance of pop and alcohol hit my nostrils. I'm sure routine spills can and do happen and every time I come here, it's all I smell.

Inside was tight quarters, but we meandered our way to the cooler and each of us came back to the counter with a diet pop.

Behind the register was a young man—or I thought it was a man. He was dressed in a skeleton costume and I couldn't stop myself from making a remark about it. "Are you expecting trick or treater's soon?"

He glanced up from the register. "Huh?"

"She means the costume," Eleanor said.

"We won't be open when that fiasco begins, fortunately, but the boss loves Halloween and not only does he allow us to dress up, but he's having a huge bash at his house that we're all invited to."

Eleanor picked up an orange flashlight from a bucket full of them. "I'll take one of these. We're staying out at the Butler Mansion and you just never know when I'll be left in the dark again."

We had his attention now as his face lit up. "Is it true what they say about that place— that it's haunted?"

"Yup," Eleanor said. "That place is chock full of ghosts—a real haunted mansion."

"How about that. I've heard the stories, but I had no idea."

"They're opening up as a bed and breakfast today, on Halloween of all days."

"No way. I'll have to check it out."

"Don't forget," Eleanor said. "The actress, Sara Knoxville, owns the place."

"You mean the one that was in a movie about a bridesmaid?" he asked. "She had a great nude scene in that movie."

I rolled my eyes. "I'd keep that to yourself if you get the chance to meet her. Saying something like that to her might make her a little nervous."

"Oh, okay. Gotcha. That'll be ten bucks."

"Ten dollars for two pops and a flashlight?"

"Well, it's not Walmart," he said with a grin.

Eleanor and I trounced back to the car and when we piled back in, I said, "Eleanor, it might be a good idea if we keep the haunted mansion thing to ourselves. It might hurt business at the Butler Mansion."

"First, it's not even open yet, and second, a haunting would be great for business. Some places rake in the bucks, and folks would line up for the opportunity to spend the night in a real haunted mansion."

"I suppose, but I'm not so sure Sara would feel that way. Her father was murdered in that mansion, don't forget."

"True. Hey, was the male ghost you saw Herman Butler?"

"I don't think so. The man I saw was dressed up in a tuxedo. It also looked like 30s era clothing. We really need to question Sara about the history of that mansion."

"Well, ship builders originally had the mansion built. I suppose it could be anyone. Do you think that suitcase Peterson found belonged to Caroline?"

"I'm not sure, but last night that closet was filled with 30s clothing. I managed to hide one of the photos from Sheriff Peterson when that suitcase hit the floor. I kicked it underneath a chair in the drawing room."

"Oh, smart move. Did you get a chance to get a good look at it?"

"No, but I hid it in my drawer. We can check it out later. After the night we had last night, it was the furthest thing from my mind."

"True that. I can't imagine what the Hill boys thought about seeing two old ladies wandering around the road wearing nightgowns in the middle of the night."

"Not sure, but they seemed to recover quite nicely."

I whipped the car around and went north on US 23, and it wasn't long before I had completely forgotten about the construction project between Tawas and Oscoda. All I could think about, as I drove no faster than thirty, was how horrible the timing was since tourists rented cottages along this strip.

I came to a stop right in front of a construction worker who held a stop sign to halt our movement. I tapped my fingers on the steering wheel as Caroline appeared in the back seat. "It's such an exciting day at the mansion," she explained. "They're decorating the place to a tee, and carloads of old people showed up to carve pumpkins."

"Thanks for the visual," I said.

Eleanor turned to look at me. "What visual?"

"Oh, Caroline popped back to tell us they're decorating the mansion and carving pumpkins."

"You must mean she came to tell *you* since I can't hear or see the supposed ghost."

I arched a brow. "Oh? You doubt my word that I can see a ghost then?"

"Maybe you can see a ghost or ghosts, but it's just plain weird listening to you having an entire conversation with a ghost that is unseen by me."

"I told you her name is Caroline."

"I really think you should go in for a checkup. You might have hit your head harder than we all think."

"Are you saying that because you're mad or because I can see someone you can't?"

"I'm not mad. I'm concerned. Who is this Caroline and what does she want?"

"We're trying to figure out who she is, remember?"

"What has she told you?"

Caroline just shook her head and faded away, thankfully, since I really would rather she not be here right now.

"I think she wants to help us with our investigations—kinda like a silent partner," I said.

"Agnes Barton, have you lost your mind? She's silent, all right, like non-existent. Besides, how can she help us since she's basically invisible to everyone except you?"

"Well, she opened the French doors the first time at the Butler Mansion, and possibly the second, although I doubt that since I believe someone might have already accessed the mansion."

"That day we found the suitcase in that bedroom with the letters?"

"Exactly."

"They might have been there before, too. Like the day we found Katherine's body."

"Are you suggesting that whoever murdered Katherine might

have been lurking in the secret passageway while the police were there?"

"Yes, and returned after we left that day, or at least returned the next day we found the suitcase."

"I suppose it sounds reasonable to think that someone took that suitcase after we found it that day, taking it before we were able to show it to the sheriff, which means someone was for *sure* lurking in that passageway or mansion about the same time we were there."

"Yes, and it could be whoever murdered Katherine."

"If she was murdered at all, Eleanor. We really need to find out what the cause of death really is."

"If she wasn't murdered, then we have an even bigger mystery."

"True, and if someone came back to the mansion there's only one reason for that—they're looking for the money."

"What money?"

"The money she swindled from Jack and Elsie."

"First, we need to establish if Jack and Elsie had an alibi for the time of Katherine's death."

I stepped on the gas, proceeding slowly as our lane had the slow sign now. It was a beautiful day with glimpses of Lake Huron from between cabins.

"If Martha can't find out how Katherine died, I'm going to ask Trooper Sales. I'd hate to do it, but he's married into my family. There has to be some fringe benefit for allowing Bill to date and marry Sophia."

Eleanor chuckled. "I hardly think it was under your control, Agnes. Sophia's a headstrong woman with her own mind."

"Believe me, I know." I recalled all too well how upset I had been at the time, but you can't stop true love. Even though there was an age difference between Sophia and Trooper Sales, their relationship has worked out just fine. They now have a bouncing baby girl to dote on and later chase the men away when she reaches dating age. I sure hoped I would still be alive to see that happen firsthand.

When we finally were free of the construction zone, I made way for Oscoda, making the turn onto Evergreen. The address led to the downtown area and as I rolled up to the white-sided house with a white picket fence, I couldn't help but notice it had New England style charm. You just don't see many homes that look like this in our neck of the woods.

I parked along the street and Eleanor and I waltzed to the door, pushing the doorbell. I body-blocked Eleanor so she couldn't keep pushing the doorbell as she had a wont to do.

When the door was answered by a woman ten years my junior, around sixty, I introduced ourselves. "Hello, are you Connie Mathews?"

She adjusted her wire-rimmed glasses. "Who's asking?"

"I'm Agnes Barton and this is—"

"Why on earth didn't you say so? Come in, come in," she said as she ushered us inside.

"I'm Eleanor Mason," El said.

"Of course you are. I've heard the two of you are legends around the East Tawas area."

"Not sure about that, but I guess we do okay."

"Outstanding sleuths, from the sounds of it."

"Yes," Eleanor said. "But we're humble. Is it true you actually worked for the sheriff's department?"

"Sure is, and believe me, it wasn't easy all those years. Two Sheriff Petersons—who knew?"

"So who did you like better, Hal or Clem Peterson?"

"Well, I had barely seen much of Hal. He had retired before I came to work there."

"I see. Well, I heard you're quite the history buff," I said, trying to stall since I hadn't a clue how to ask Connie if she had a basement full of old newspapers."

"Spit it out, old girl. I'd be honored if I could help you two out."

"Newspapers," Eleanor said. "We heard you collect old newspapers."

Connie's face lit up. "I sure do. Follow me and I'll show you my collection."

She led the way across her wood floors and stopped at a white door, pulling a skeleton key from around her neck that was on a chain. Connie clattered the key in the lock until it snapped open. "Watch your steps, ladies."

I took a tight hold of the handrail and descended the rickety steps, reminding Eleanor to be extra careful. Connie flicked the lights on and my mouth flew open, a fist finding its way inside. All along the walls were newspaper clippings and mug shots.

"Wow, you're a real crackpot," Eleanor blurted out.

"What my partner means is that you have quite the collection. Are these unsolved cases?"

"Yup. Most of them are quite old since Iosco County is relatively safe these days, but you'd be surprised how many unsolved cases there really are."

Dead center was a newspaper article by the Iosco County Herald, with a story about Sheriff Charles C. Miller who lost his life in the line of duty, July first, 1934.

"I had no idea an Iosco County sheriff lost his life. How awful," I said.

"Yes, it was quite awful, but that was way before my time."

"Then why hang it here? It reads that they found the culprit."

"Yes, but it's a very historic event."

"True." I stared at the other newspaper articles with photos of both men and women. "Not many murders here."

"No, but there are a variety of crimes, including the murder of the Robinson's."

"That case was solved," I said.

"By us," El added. "It turned out to be—"

"We're here to find out what you might have about a possibly murdered or missing woman by the name of Caroline."

Connie rocked back on her heels. "I see." She stared at the photos on the wall, but then went to a stack of tubs piled four tall, each labeled with years. "What year are we talking here?"

"1930."

Connie picked up a tub and set it down on a table in the far corner. "You can start there, but if it was any unsolved crime, I'd have the article on the wall."

I opened the tub and wrinkled my nose. I lifted each newspaper out and Eleanor cocked a brow at me. Each was covered with tight-fitting plastic as a way to preserve the brown paper. After all, 1930 was a long time ago.

Eleanor chuckled. "Looks like we'll be here all day."

I grimaced, as that was so *not* what I wanted to hear. "Keep looking, Eleanor."

I lifted newspaper after newspaper from the box, searching each of them. When I had taken them all out and scanned each of them, I loaded them back in, and moved the tub to the floor.

Right on cue, another tub quickly took its place by the diligent Connie. "I told you it wouldn't be easy."

"More like looking for a needle in a haystack," Eleanor said.

I again took the pains to remove the newspapers while Eleanor read them with a tilt of her head since she wore bifocals and the poor dear didn't have sense enough to look through her glasses the right way. The problem with that was your eyes only got worse.

Connie disappeared and returned with a pot of hot water and empty cups, tea bags displayed prominently on the tray. We continued to work as the cups were filled and Eleanor assisted by dunking tea bags into the hot water.

When I finished the tub, Connie piled the newspapers back

inside, bringing a new tub. "Enjoy your tea, Agnes. You girls sure are determined."

I took a sip of my tea and grimaced. "What on earth, Eleanor?"

"What?" she asked in innocence. "It's green tea, a great anti-oxidant."

I made another face. "Why is it that everything good for you has to taste so bad?"

"Beats me, Aggie, but at our age, we need to at least try to be healthier, and that means making better food choices," Eleanor insisted.

I had to laugh at that. "You mean like eating at the KFC?"

"Yes, but if we don't go there, how else will we get our tidbits of information from Ella?"

I drained the last of my tea and said, "I guess we'll never have that problem since we'll still be regulars there." Actually, from my last recollect, Ella had spilled the beans about where we were going to the other seniors we know. Sometimes it would be nice if we could make our rounds before having our friends show up so unexpectedly.

I went back to sorting through more newspapers, until finally Eleanor held up a newspaper like it was a golden ticket to the Willie Wonka's Chocolate Factory. "I found something of interest."

"Not more rummage sales ads or bake sale announcements, I hope."

"Nope," she said, handing me the paper. "It's a hit and run."

I grabbed the paper, my hands shaking now as I read out loud, "A woman in her early 30s was run down while crossing US 23, and heading toward the pier. Her name was Caroline Bellows." I waited for a moment to compose myself before I continued, "It says the woman was found sprawled out in the middle of the road."

"Was the light red when she crossed?" Eleanor asked.

"I'm not sure. It doesn't say, but I'm also not so sure they had traffic lights here back then."

Caroline appeared behind Eleanor and smiled sadly. Instead of looking black and white, she had more color to her. I could see her silver headband, green dress and pearls that were dangling around her neck.

"It was late that day and I never saw the car coming," Caroline said.

"Can you give us a few moments, Connie?" I said, wanting to get rid of her so I could speak with Caroline privately.

"Caroline's here now," I whispered to Eleanor.

"I'll let you speak privately to her then since you can hear her and I can't," Eleanor said sadly.

Caroline laughed, the sound echoing in the basement. Eleanor clutched my arm tightly, "I think I can s-see dead people, too."

"Oh, poo," Caroline said. "You can see me because I want you to."

Eleanor trembled. "Why? I don't think I want to see any gh-ghosts."

"I can't imagine most people really want to see an actual ghost. Of course, at first they act like they want to, until one shows up."

"I don't have a problem with Agnes seeing a ghost."

"That's not what you said in the car earlier, but don't worry, Eleanor, I don't want to take your place, silly heart. We all need to work as a team. Now that you have figured out how I died, if you two put your heads together, you can figure out why I'm still here. Why I never moved on."

"What do you remember about that day?"

"Just that I was in a hurry, but I can't remember why."

"So you never saw the car?" Eleanor asked.

"Nope. All I know is the car was traveling fast, and when it struck me, everything went black. I must have been killed instantly."

"That's what it says in the paper," Agnes said. "Perhaps you died so suddenly that you never realized it."

"You said everything went black," Eleanor began. "But how long were you out? Didn't you realize you were dead?"

"No, not at first I didn't. I woke up in the middle of the road got up and ran to the side of the road. It was then that I saw the ambulance and my body laying there."

"That must have been just awful," I said with a shake of my head.

"It was. When the ambulance sped away, it never occurred to me that I should follow it."

Eleanor wrinkled up her face. "So you didn't see a light or anybody coming for you?"

"Not at all. All I could think about was how I sure got the bad end of the stick."

"What did you do after the ambulance left? Did you go anywhere all these years?"

"I tried, but I could only go as far as the side of the street. I stood there for many years watching tourists bustle on the streets and trains roaring past. East Tawas changed and I was just stuck here, watching it all happen. When I saw Agnes' car roar past, I tried to tell her to slow down, that another car was on a collision course with her, but she didn't see me. When those cars collided, I was thrown into the passenger's seat and was along for the ride. The ambulance came and this time, I was allowed to leave with it and Agnes."

"So you weren't able to leave before, but suddenly you could," Eleanor said. "Were you run over in the same spot Agnes had the accident?"

"Exactly the same place. Look, I'm not sure how this whole ghost thing works. All I know is, that I was able to go where Agnes went, like the hospital. I wasn't sure if she'd be able to see me or not, but when she buried her head under the blanket I knew she did. When she was still unconscious, I felt like the angel of death. I expected she'd die and we'd be able to transition to the next stop or to the everlasting life. Being a ghost is no fun, especially when you're all alone."

"If you weren't able to leave before," I began, "then how are you able to disappear at will, and travel to other locations like the Butler Mansion when I'm not even there?"

"Sorry, I can't help you there. I really don't understand how this whole dead thing works. I almost wonder if I had that ability long ago, but never knew it."

"Do you have a family?" Eleanor asked. "Or—"

"The thing is that I can remember few details. Until you ladies found that newspaper article, I didn't remember how I died, or much of anything else."

"And now?" I asked.

"Well, now I can't remember much except my accident. I don't know why, but I have the feeling that whoever did this to me has passed on."

"What about the ghost at the Butler Mansion? The man I saw you chasing through a wall yesterday?"

"Actually, Agnes, I just don't know. All I know is that I wanted to speak to him. None of the ghosts at the mansion will speak to me."

"How many gh-ghosts are there?" Eleanor stuttered.

"Well, I'm not sure the exact number, but there's one woman who lives in the attic. She's a bit grumpy and chased me out when I visited. She told me she doesn't like my type. I'm still not sure what that means."

"So a man and a woman," I said. "I sure hope they decide to behave themselves when the mansion opens as a bed and breakfast."

Eleanor drank her tea. "Perhaps you could ask them to, Caroline."

"I suppose I could try, but like I said, they don't talk to me."

"Perhaps you need to make them listen to you," I suggested.

"I'll try right now," Carolina said as she faded away in a puff of smoke.

Connie's eyes opened wide when she joined us. "I knew I shouldn't have allowed you girls to go through those newspapers.

It's so thick down here. Did you g-girls see that black smoke down here? I sure hope a g-ghost won't decide to take up residence in my basement now."

"Smoke? No. You see any smoke, Eleanor?"

"Nope, but I'm sure ready to head back to East Tawas and maybe check out how things went for Martha,"

I offered to help Connie straighten up the basement, but she shooed us away. I personally was happy with a few things. I knew more about Caroline than I once did, and now I didn't have to hide the truth from Eleanor.

CHAPTER TWELVE

I called Martha and she told me she was home, so Eleanor and I made our way there. Parked alongside my trailer was a black car that I believed belonged to the coroner, Walter Smitty.

"Oh, boy," Eleanor said as we jumped from the car after it screeched to a halt. I heard a panting sound, but when I didn't see a hellhound, I remembered that Leotyne's pooch had met its end and that his ghost had chased Caroline up a tree.

I hadn't made it ten feet before I heard a growling and snapping at my feet, but for some reason, the ghost of a dog isn't nearly as menacing as the real thing, so I ignored him.

Eleanor was the one who rapped on the door, and a red-faced Martha stuck her head out. She quickly ushered us inside and whispered, "Help, I can't get him to leave."

"Did you find out anything yet?"

"Are you kidding me? I've been battling his advances ever since he arrived."

I strode over to Walter and said, "Hello, there. I'm not sure if you remember me or not."

He downed the contents of his shot glass. "Oh, yes—the investigator."

"Investigators," Eleanor piped up. "What are you doing here?"

"Martha invited me, but I didn't expect anyone else to arrive. I sure hope you haven't brought that Sheriff Peterson with you."

"Of course not. What makes you think he'd be here?"

"Well, it seems like we have a difference of opinion. I know he's the sheriff and all, but I've never been asked to withhold autopsy results before. Why, do you know he released information that he's still investigating Katherine's death, or I should say Barbara Billings?"

"Barbara Billings?" I asked in shock.

"Yes, she's the woman you found at the mansion. It seems she was using an alias, or so the sheriff says." He poured himself another shot. "I know I shouldn't be divulging this information since he's investigating, but she wasn't murdered."

I flopped on the seat opposite Walter. "You don't say? Well, what did her in then?"

"Heart attack I suspect, but there really was no sign of clogged arteries to speak of. I've seen a case like this some years back, but that defied reason, too."

"And the toxicology reports?"

"All came back clear. I even checked to see if she had been given any insulin. I had a case years ago where someone gave a healthy patient insulin and it caused them to go into cardiac arrest. By the time she arrived at the hospital, she was too far gone to be revived."

"So did the sheriff tell you why he wanted the results kept quiet?"

"He wanted to investigate more since she was suspected of running a stock scam. It seems she's victimized quite a number of residents in Tawas."

"Oh, I know, and thanks for the information. I sure would never get that juicy of a tidbit from Peterson, that's for sure."

"Don't tell him I told you so, please."

"I sure won't."

"Has anyone claimed the remains yet?"

"That's the strangest thing … no. So either they don't know, or are too worried if they're involved in her criminal activity."

I sighed. "I just don't understand any of this. I had hoped to get some kind of clue, but I haven't come up with anything. This information has cleared the names of some of my friends that were scammed by Katherine."

"She has ties to Bay Port, in the thumb in Michigan, or that's what her driver's license that Trooper Sales found said."

"Is there anything else you could tell me?"

He leaned closer to me. "How does a man get close to your daughter, Martha? I had thought she was raring to go, and once we got here she gave me the cold shoulder."

"She's like that. Actually, she dates younger men for the most part."

He squared his shoulders. "That explains it. I might as well head home, then."

"One more question from a medical standpoint. Is it possible for someone to be scared to death?"

He stood. "It's quite possible if the person was truly frightened enough that it could trigger an overflow of adrenaline that would cause the heart to go into abnormal rhythms that just can't sustain life. They'd essentially drop dead."

"Did you find evidence of that during autopsy?"

"The heart didn't look damaged at all, but this is a plausible cause of death. I've listed it as a heart attack. It was brought on by unknown circumstances, in my opinion, since her heart didn't seem to have any defects."

That made so much sense to me. "Thanks."

"I'd love to know what you two find out. Like what caused Katherine's heart attack. What would frighten her so bad? It might explain the fingernail marks on her neck. She must have grabbed her neck when she went into distress. I imagine by then she was having difficulty breathing. Not as interesting a death as caused by a vampire, like you both thought. Actually, that would have been a more interesting case," he chuckled. "One for the record books you might say, eh?"

I would have laughed, but I felt it was one of those jokes someone who does autopsies for a living might tell, so I just nodded.

We waited until Walter was out the door before I began to pace. "We can't run to Bay Port now. There simply isn't time. We're expected back at the mansion by five."

"I could make a few calls, or check her Facebook account," Eleanor suggested.

Martha brought out her laptop and Eleanor's fingers flew on the keyboard, searching Katherine's name and her alias. Both pages seemed quite similar, with one eerie coincidence; there was a man on her friend's list that resembled the man who kidnapped Stuart and me! I went to his page, but wasn't able to see any information. He certainly didn't have the name Len McGroovy like he told me his name was. His profile name was Peyton Murphy. It listed his address as Bay Port, Michigan.

"Martha, where is Stuart?"

"Oh, how would I know? He's undercover, you know. He wouldn't tell me the particulars, but he did say that visiting you at the hospital wasn't the only reason he was in town."

My face fell. "That's disappointing. I imagined as much since the last time I saw him, he was spying on someone at the beach. We were even kidnapped when the man confronted him, or I should say us."

"What on earth?" Eleanor said. "When did this happen?"

"That day I left you with Martha. I lied to you about going to see Dr. Thomas that day, but I did tell you I was trying to find Stuart. Well, I found him and got myself into the middle of Stuart's investigation."

Martha put the whiskey bottle to her lips and took a swig. "I think I need a nip for this story."

"I whacked the woman in the head."

"What woman?" Eleanor asked as Martha took another drink.

"Stuart's wife. She's a lovely woman except for the holding a gun on me part. After I knocked her out, we rolled out of the moving van."

"Why weren't you hospitalized after that?" Martha wanted to know.

"The van wasn't moving all that fast yet."

"I see. Well, you've had quite an adventure already. What else have you been up to without anyone knowing?"

"She sees dead people. I mean ghosts," Eleanor added. "We're trying to unravel the story, but it looks like there's an even bigger mystery at hand."

Martha laughed. "Seeing ghosts isn't enough for you two?"

"Nope. Since Katherine died of natural causes, we have to wonder what that Len character is looking for. I personally have to wonder where Katherine stuffed all the money that she swindled out of everyone, or mainly, Jack Winston and Elsie Bradford."

Martha took another drink and choked on it. Eleanor promptly trotted over and gave her a pat on the back. Once she was able to talk again, she continued. "I suppose you two had better get moving, It's already four o'clock. You'll have to sort all of this out later. If you don't get back to the mansion soon, Sara might have one of those Hollywood wig-out moments."

I did one final search on Facebook for International Energy, but instead of finding a picture of that Len McGroovy character listed as president under his alias, Katherine was listed as president.

"There's a page for International Energy," I informed Eleanor and Martha who then gathered behind me, reading the screen. "I suppose they needed to have a page just in case someone checked them out." I hit the link on their 'about' page, stating it was a website, but it ended up with a broken link. "It seems they don't have a website anymore."

"Maybe it's bankrupt just like Jack told Elsie," Eleanor said.

I nodded and lit out the door, more in a hurry than ever before. I had to check this out and possibly find the cash I was convinced was hidden at the mansion. It was clear now why Len was in town and why someone might be investigating him—like my son. Eleanor and I buckled in and the ghost dog hopped in the back seat, yapping up a storm.

I sighed and backed out.

"What's wrong with you?"

"You remember that hellhound of Leotyne's?" When Eleanor bobbed her head in agreement, I added, "He's dead and is a ghost now. He's riding in the backseat."

"So now we have a ghost dog to add to our list of crazy things going on?"

"So it appears."

Instead of Eleanor remarking about that, she gripped her purse with both hands while the car jetted toward the Butler Mansion.

Chapter Thirteen

I rolled up the drive of the Butler Mansion and Caroline appeared in the backseat of the car before it came to a halt, but the ghost dog took one look at her and chased her from the car.

I got out and sauntered toward the porch where there was a red carpet rolled out for guests to enter. Lit jack-o'-lanterns decorated with horrific carved faces sat on the steps, and well, basically, all over the porch. I carefully ascended the few steps and Elsie greeted me.

"I was wondering if you girls would ever get here. Sara arrived ten minutes ago and was fussing about you two not being here. We told her you went out to get ice cream." When I gave her a look, she added, "Well, it seemed like a good enough idea at the time."

"Not a problem, dear. We were doing a little investigating and found out the best tidbit of information that cleared both you and Jack Winston, but we'll have to keep it to ourselves for now. I'm sure the sheriff hasn't wrapped up his end of it just yet."

"Tell me about it. He was out to question me this morning."

"What did he say?"

"Just wanted to know the how and why of handing over the cash to Katherine. It seems she had an alias, but Peterson was still trying to hash out the details. He also told me that I was cleared as a suspect in Katherine's death, but he wouldn't tell me how or why. That man sure can be tight-lipped at times."

I had to agree on that, but lucky for us, the coroner wasn't a bit close-lipped.

"There are costumes on your beds for you to change into. I haven't seen 30s era clothing in quite some time, but my mother sure had a chest full of it. It was great for playing dress up," Elsie explained.

I raised a brow, and Eleanor and I went in search of the costumes that she spoke about. When I walked into my room, Caroline was hiding behind the door. "That ghost dog won't quit. I had quite the time losing him."

"I see. Well, where did these costumes come from?" I asked, indicating the black flapper dress that was lying on my bed.

"I thought you might like it."

I picked it up and admired the sequins and fringe. "I love it. Thanks, Caroline."

Once I had dressed and strolled into the hallway, Eleanor surfaced from her room dressed in a matching flapper dress—hers in red—that made her skin appear even more pale than normal. To make up for it, bright rouge was smeared on both of her cheeks with blue eye shadow swept on her eyelids.

Eleanor adjusted her headband appropriately and asked, "What do you think?"

I thought how much I really wanted to take a better look at the picture hidden in my drawer, but with Caroline lurking so close, I didn't think it was the best of ideas. I couldn't help but wonder if Caroline knew more than she was letting on.

"Looks great, but I must say that Caroline was responsible for our costumes."

"How, I wonder?"

"Beats me, Eleanor, but she might have clothing on hand. Last time I checked, there was a closet full of it in the room where Peterson found that suitcase."

Eleanor strode up the hallway and waltzed into the room, whipping open the door of the closet, but instead of the 30s clothing I had seen earlier, two people yanked us from behind. A lever was then pushed and we were all propelled into the corridor hidden behind the wall.

The beam of the flashlight shone in my eyes and I blinked repeatedly. Sure enough, it was Len McGroovy and the female I had knocked unconscious the other day.

"Great, this has worked out much better than I had hoped," Len said. "Now you can help us."

"Help you how?" I asked.

"Help us find the money, of course. Katherine has been holding back for some time. I worked out the deal with her some time ago, but instead of turning the money over to me, she decided to swindle me, too."

"Well, Len. That's just awful, but it really has nothing to do with me."

"Us," chimed in Eleanor. "She keeps forgetting about me."

The woman took a hold of my arm. "Hey, now. Aren't you my daughter in-law?"

"Stuart really needs to keep his yap shut."

I wished I could take it back when Len pulled a gun from his belt and pointed it at the woman. "Is that right, Mona? Are you plotting against me?"

"Of course not! We're a team, remember?"

"I don't recall saying that exactly. Now that I to think about it, you let Stuart and his loud-mouthed mother go."

"I did not. She attacked me with her purse. I was knocked out."

"Your purse, Aggie?" Eleanor asked. "Whatever did you have inside it?"

"Rolled coins—like, thirty dollars' worth."

"Smart move. I personally like to carry a pistol, but unfortunately I've left it back in my room."

"Enough with the jibber jabber," Len threatened. "Get moving, the three of you."

"I swear, Len. I've not betrayed you."

"And I suppose you'll tell me you don't work for the FBI, either."

"I ... I ... No."

Some special agent she was, caving like that. "I'm sure she's no good, just like you, Len."

"We've been all over this place and there isn't any money," Eleanor added.

"Well, if that's the case, I'll kill you right here."

I gulped. "There're a few places we haven't looked, I suppose," I said. "But the mansion will be full soon since it's the grand opening of the bed and breakfast."

"Which makes me wonder why Katherine would hole up here."

"Perfect cover, I suppose. If she hadn't died so unexpectedly, we'd have been working with her to ready the mansion, but I suppose since you murdered her, you'll never find the money."

"I didn't murder her. I was here that day, but she was long gone when I found her upstairs on the third floor."

My wheels turned. The third floor is the same floor that Eleanor and I had seen a ghost walking toward, or at least that's where I felt she was going. "So how exactly did she get from the third floor to the main floor?"

"I didn't want the cops tearing up that third floor room. They might have found the money if she had hidden it there. I barely escaped that day"

"Did you check the room where she was staying?"

"Of course I did, but I had to make my great escape when the cops showed up. Luckily, Katherine had told me about the secret passageway she found."

I glanced around. "I suppose the money might be in here somewhere."

"My bet is on the third floor," Eleanor suggested. "Of course, it's dangerous up there. I wonder how Katherine really died."

I could see where Eleanor was going with this. Eleanor had nearly lost her life in that room. That was, until the ghosts of the Butler Mansion had other plans. They had warned me that day, and I had freed Eleanor from the ropes before she could be propelled out the window to her death. Yes, we had to get Len up there. If Katherine had been frightened to death, perhaps Len could be, too.

"Hand over your pistol, Mona," Len said in a menacing tone. "I'm not about to let you get the drop on me."

"Len, you can't think that I actually work for the FBI. You always said I'm not that bright."

"I beg to differ. You're smarter than I gave you credit for. Convincing a couple of old bats to help you is one for the record books."

"I'm not—"

"We're not," I added.

"Besides, she already pulled a gun on Stuart and me once. You can't think we'd be in cahoots with her," I said.

"Would you all just shut up? We're going go back through the passageway and make our way to the third floor. If Katherine had died there, she must have hidden something up there."

"Unless she heard noises," Eleanor added. "You do know this place is majorly haunted, don't you?"

"I've been in and out of this place on many occasions, including that day you two showed up—the day after Katherine died. I hid in the passageway that day, too. Lucky for me, I was able to slip from the mansion undetected."

"Was it you who took the suitcase we found that day?"

"Yes, but it didn't have anything in it but clothing."

He was slick, this one. He had hidden in the passageway while Eleanor and I were going through Katherine's suitcase, and stole it while we were outside with the sheriff. That really gave me the chills. Eleanor and I were in more danger that day than we realized.

"So you're quite an escape artist," I said. "If you try to escape now you'll probably get away. If not, my son, Stuart, will show up to make the arrest. You'll wind up in some prison cell."

"Federal prison is a piece of cake next to the state prison system, but I won't be seeing any prison cell after I find the money. You'll all be quite dead, though."

"Isn't running a Ponzi scheme enough of an offense?"

"Actually, Katherine was the one running the scheme. You won't find my name anywhere, and if I let any of you live, I'll go down for sure."

He pushed us ahead of him and whispered that if any of us said a word, he'd kill us on the spot. I noted that his revolver had a silencer, so I wasn't willing to risk his threats, nor put the lives of my friends downstairs into jeopardy. I prayed that they wouldn't come looking for us upstairs.

We silently moved into the room and up the hallway to the stairs that led to the third floor. Caroline appeared and led the way like she knew where we were going. I wanted to scream for her to do something, anything, to show herself, but she's just a ghost, after all, and I can't see any ghost frightening Len to death like one may have frightened Katherine.

Eleanor and I climbed the steps first and kept to the back of the room, far from the third floor window from which several people had fallen to their deaths. Of course, now there should not be anything to cause anyone to fall from the window, unless they were pushed.

Len instructed us to begin our search and we started with the bookshelves nearest to us, flopping books to the floor with a loud bang. I then shrugged as Len pointed his gun menacingly toward me.

"Do something," I said to Caroline.

"What am I supposed to do? I'm a ghost."

"Rattle something like you did the dining room table."

"Who are you talking to?" Len asked.

"Caroline, she's a ghost. She sorta attached herself to me when I had a car accident."

He laughed. "You really are off your rocker. Everyone knows there is no such thing as—"

"Ghosts?" I said.

Try as I might, I knew that I wouldn't be able to will ghosts to appear. This was one of those moments when I knew we were in dire straits. If something didn't happen, and quick, we'd all be goners.

The shelf across from us began to rattle, knocking a jar down. When it smashed to the floor, three apparitions appeared, one of which became a black mist that bounced off wall after wall with a wailing sound. Eleanor and I hugged each other, not because I was afraid of the ghosts. Quite the contrary. I felt they were trying to help us, although the way Len was waving his pistol bothered me to no end. I certainly hoped that he didn't think bullets would stop ghosts.

"It's a banshee," Eleanor shrieked.

"Make it stop!" he screamed.

"You make it stop. There's no such thing as ghosts, remember?"

His eyes bulged and he cracked off a shot. Mona knocked us to the ground, sheltering us with her body, but I watched from beneath one of her arms as the bullet ricocheted, striking Len in the middle of his forehead. The three ghosts hovered for a moment, one of them saying, "Serves you right for disturbing us." They then turned into a black mist and disappeared into a picture of two elderly ladies and an old man, none of whom I recognized.

"I bet those are the same ghosts that helped us the last time," I said. Staring down at the broken jar and dust, I added, "This might be their ashes."

"Oh, no. All Butler descendants have to be buried in the cemetery, remember?"

"I completely forgot about that, Eleanor."

Mona stood up and helped us up as well. "I'm so glad you ladies are unhurt. I sure wouldn't want to try and explain to Stuart about how I had allowed his mother to be murdered."

"So you do work for the FBI after all?"

"Yes, I've been undercover for quite a while. Stuart—"

Before she could say anything further, Andrew and Stuart burst into the room, each wanting to save the day for totally different reasons. Andrew, because I was his beloved, and Stuart, because he was on the case of a Ponzi scheme that involved both Katherine and Len.

"Are you okay, Agnes?" Andrew asked, taking me into his arms.

"Oh, yes, but you sure could have gotten here sooner. On second thought, I'm glad you didn't, but how did you know I was in danger?"

"When I arrived and couldn't find either or you, I just knew something was amiss, but then I heard the gunshot ... I knew you were in trouble. I ran into Stuart on the way up here."

"Mona's wearing a wire," Stuart explained. "It was hardly the time to tell Andrew to stay back, but I have an idea he wouldn't have listened anyway."

"You got that right, Stuart," Andrew said.

Mona patted Stuart on the back. "Your mother is one smart cookie. I'd work with her anytime."

Stuart rubbed his neck. "Please don't encourage her. I've been trying to convince her to give up her investigative ways."

Mona chuckled at that. "Len has been coming back here to look for the money that Katherine had swindled, but it appears he didn't have anything to do with her death. He admitted that when he found her, she was already dead."

"You weren't with him that day?" I asked.

"No. I was back at the motel. I hadn't met up with him until later that day."

"So how did she die?" Stuart asked.

"Actually, I believe she was scared to death. We spoke to the coroner and he admitted that she died of natural causes. He told us it was completely plausible that she had died from an excess of adrenalin."

Stuart scratched his head. "She died how?"

"Adrenaline overload," Mona said. "I've heard about it, but I never heard of anyone who was verified of dying that way. I wonder if Len showing up caused her to die. He was the one in charge of funneling funds though a third party, but it looks like we've really hit the wall this time. I doubt that Len has any incriminating documents that would tell us if anyone else was involved."

"He's too smart for that," I agreed. "He even mentioned that his name wasn't on anything." So was this the end of it or not? "I'm thinking that Katherine was scared to death because she saw a ghost. Since she was up here, just maybe the money is hidden up here somewhere."

Stuart shook his head. "A what? Ghost, you say? There's no such thing as—"

"Shhh," Eleanor and I said, echoing one another. "You wouldn't like to see them, I assure you. When Len fired a shot at the ghosts though, it ricocheted and killed him dead."

"I see. I think I'll leave the ghost part out of my report, if you don't mind."

"I can write it up excluding the mention," Mona said. "By the way, my real name is Moraine."

"Our friends, Jack Winston and Elsie Bradford, were both conned out of their money." I went on to say the exact amounts, and Stuart made a call via his cell. Soon sirens were sounding off as cop cars tore into the driveway. I wanted to stay and help Stuart look for the money, but they shooed us off.

By the time we had made it downstairs, the first trick or treaters were at the door. Sara sauntered her way there, giving a clown and cowboy two large candy bars each and, just like the proper actress, she never let them see her sweat.

Sheriff Peterson strode in the door asking what happened, and I explained to him as best I could—excluding the ghost part.

"So how did Katherine really die?" I asked Peterson.

"Coroner says it was natural causes, heart attack."

I stared him down. "Why did the news report that there was on ongoing investigation?"

"Well, when we found out she wasn't who we thought she was, we put everything on hold. We really were trying to figure out who she was. I had no idea there was an ongoing FBI investigation until much later. I wasn't at liberty to discuss the case further. Unfortunately, the coroner didn't understand that."

"I see. I can't say I blame him entirely, but I suppose he has a job to do and so do you."

Caroline was nowhere in sight and I really wondered if she'd found her way to the other side, but there was so much more I had to check out.

Sara's eyes now were quite wide and I asked her if she was okay.

"Okay? A man was murdered upstairs and you expect me to be okay? I'll be lucky if this place makes it a year. Who wants to spend the night in a murder house?"

"It's already been a murder house, Sara," I said. "And Len's death was accidental. If he hadn't cracked off that shot, it would never have ricocheted and killed him."

"What did it ricochet off of anyway?" Trooper Sales asked as he lingered in the background.

"Beats me. I'm just glad that Eleanor and I will live to tell the tale."

Caroline's absence really began to bother me, and I went in search of her just as Mona and Stuart came up the stairs, bringing the cops with them to the third floor. I wasn't sure, but I hoped the ghosts—whoever they were—decided to play nice and stay inside the picture frame from which they were wont to appear. All I knew was that they'd saved us in a big way once again.

CHAPTER FOURTEEN

I stared at the picture frame with interest. The man wore a black tuxedo from the 30s era. His hair was slicked back and he had a twinkle in his eyes. I sat in the drawing room while everyone else was in the dining room chatting. The cops had left hours ago, an ambulance carting off Len's body to the morgue. After over half an hour, Sara batted her eyelashes the right way while speaking to Sheriff Peterson so that the mansion wouldn't be considered a crime scene. After a thorough search of the third floor, no money was found. Stuart and Moraine, along with a slew of federal agents, convened on the cemetery after the money wasn't found in the mansion. Luckily, they left the mansion intact. Andrew made sure of that, claiming his client, Sara, had been through quite enough already.

"Who are you?" I asked the man.

I felt a breeze move my hair slightly and I looked up, making my way to the window. When I glanced outside, I saw a van parked well away from the mansion, and with my iPhone in hand, I made my way outside. An owl hooted nearby as I approached the van, my cell's flashlight my only resource. When I was at the van, I cupped my hands around my face, trying to see inside. In was then that the door moved slightly. I tried the door and found it was unlocked. My nostrils flared at the chemical smell inside, and after I swept my flashlight along the interior, I realized this van belonged to the cleaners. It was then that I also caught sight of a wheelchair. It would seem that Robert wasn't as wheelchair-bound as he seemed. His wheelchair was here, but he wasn't.

I hurried back to the mansion, noting the lights coming from the third floor window. I should have known all along that the cleaners weren't who they said they were. They'd been searching for the money the whole time! Katherine had accomplices after all, and they might just find something the cops missed.

I called Stuart and told him to get back to the mansion and pronto. I didn't stay on the line to listen to him say for me to wait for him. They might get away before he got here, and I just couldn't risk it. Caroline tried to block my way on the stairs, but I ran right through her. I retrieved Eleanor's pistol as I heard loud noises coming from the third floor. I was on my own now, just me and Caroline, who was glued to my side.

"Agnes, don't go up there alone."

"I don't have a choice. Stuart is on his way. I can't let them get away."

I slid Eleanor's revolver in my pocket for safekeeping, and slowly moved up the stairs. Larry held a flashlight for Gary, who had a mallet and chisel and was hammering away between the bricks of the wall that protruded out about a foot. Although this room had no fireplace, the chimney loomed directly over it on the roof.

"Hurry up," Robert shouted. "It won't be long before those old bats will be coming upstairs for bed."

"I'm trying, but how can't they be hearing all this pounding up here?"

My thoughts were that it was because this house was built solid as a rock with thick walls, but if they didn't hurry, someone might just discover what they were doing. "I'd check to see if a brick was loose, personally," I said out loud, then clapped my mouth with my hand.

The three men stopped what they were doing and stared over to where I stood with the quivering Caroline. "Here we go again."

I moved my hand down and asked, "So you're Katherine's accomplices?"

Robert pulled out a gun, pointing it at me. "She's my sister, or was before she died. I wasn't involved in her schemes, but she spilled the beans when I saw her with wads of cash. She refused to bring me in, so after her death I came here to locate the money she conned out of those people."

"Did she also tell you where the money is?"

"No, but since that man came here to search in this room, it has to be in here. We overheard the cops arguing about not being able to lock down the scene, and luckily the feds are now looking elsewhere."

Caroline wailed. "Oh, no!

When I looked to see what she was looking at, I saw only a blank space, but then a black mist rose to the ceiling near the window, taking the shape of a man with sharp jagged teeth. I'm not sure if it was my expression or not, but the mallet and chisel fell to the floor with a bang, and the men ran screaming from the room, their heavy footsteps pounding on the stairs as they descended. I watched from the window, smiling in satisfaction as the feds were now here, rounding them up and ushering them to cars.

I wasn't too concerned about the black mist that floated nearby. It pointed out one specific brick and had disappeared by the time Stuart raced into the room.

"Mother, are you okay?"

"O-Oh yes," I stammered. I pointed out a brick. "You might want to search behind that brick. Robert, one of the cleaners that Sara hired, was the brother of the woman who called herself Katherine. He took the job here to find the money Katherine had hidden."

"Why that brick? It looks like they were searching above that area."

I took a hold of Stuart's shirt. "Trust me, check that brick."

I refused to leave while more feds piled into the room and hammered away at the bricks until one large chunk was lowered to the floor. A man then shined a flashlight inside, coming back with a large trash bag. He handed it to Stuart who yanked out a wad of cash rolled up with a rubber bands wound around it.

"Looks like we found the mother load," Stuart said.

When he showed me the inside of the bag, I was overwhelmed. I had to say, "That looks like more money than what Jack Winston and Elsie Bradford handed over to Katherine."

"Barbara Billings, you mean. Katherine was just an alias."

"Really?" I asked as if I had no idea. "Is it only me, or does Barbara Billings sound like an alias, or actress's name? Wasn't Billings the last name of the *Leave it to Beaver* mom?"

"No, that was Billingsley," Sara said as she waltzed into the room. She then nodded to Stuart. "Find what you're looking for finally, handsome?"

"Yes, looks that way. Sorry to be bothering you again so soon."

Sara rubbed a hand down Stuart's arm. "Not a problem. When you're done, why don't you come on down for a drink? Elsie Bradford made the most marvelous spiked lemonade."

All eyes were on Stuart now, who calmly explained, "That's against the FBI policy, I'm afraid. Besides, my wife is the jealous type."

Moraine, his wife, cleared her throat. I hadn't noticed her.

Sara's hand flew to her mouth. "I … I'm sorry. I had no idea he was married. I'd love to treat you both to dinner sometime."

"Like my husband said, it's really against policy."

"I hope you don't think I meant to hire a woman of questionable scruples?" Sara said.

"Well, did you?" I asked.

"Not at all. I put an ad on Craig's list and screened all candidates. Since Katherine lived in Michigan, she seemed like the best person for the job, and for the most part she helped me out."

"Craig's List?" I said. "That's the worst place to hire someone off of."

"Unless you do a background check," Stuart added. "So is that who hired the cleaners? Katherine?"

"Yes, she handled all the preparations and Andrew recommended that Agnes and Eleanor oversee things. I had no idea they had planned to look into Katherine's death for the most part," Sara explained.

"Yes, my mother and her meddling partner, Eleanor, know a thing or two about solving mysteries. If it wasn't for my mother tonight, the cleaners would have found and made off with the money."

"I don't believe that Robert was involved in his sister's crimes. He just came along after the fact. You can't blame him for wanting to find that money."

"I suppose not, but if he knew what his sister was doing, he should have contacted the police instead of searching for the money with the intent to take it for himself. He pulled a gun on you, Mother."

"He did, but I just feel like he was desperate. His sister had just died and it was a crime of opportunity."

"We'll be looking into what Robert really knew and when. If he had no connection to his sister's illegal activities, he won't have any worries. He's actually fortunate Len didn't find out what he was up to. Len was the real deal, a dangerous man."

"Yup," I said. "One who lost his life in this very room. On Facebook he had an alias, Peyton Murphy."

"That Robert and his cohorts came outside blabbering that they saw a demon up here," Moraine said with a snicker.

"Ghosts, now demons?" asked Sara. "I'm not sure I'm ready to run a bed and breakfast that is haunted. Whatever will the customers think?"

"That this place is haunted. I highly suspect that you'll never have a vacancy if word gets out."

"That's good, but we shouldn't really play the whole haunted mansion up."

"I'm with you on that. Let's go downstairs, Sara. I'm really ready for a glass of lemonade after the day I've had. I've had a gun pointed at me twice today."

"I tried to tell you to wait and let us handle the cleaners on the phone," Stuart said. "But I don't blame you for doing what you did. Without you, we'd be searching all night for that money."

I led Sara from the room and once we were in the dining room, I explained to everyone what had happened upstairs, wondering where Andrew was.

"So you saw a real demon up there, Agnes?" Elsie asked with a shudder.

"Not exactly sure what I saw. I just knew that it meant me no harm."

Eleanor gave me a hug and whispered, "I don't blame you for not bringing me, but next time, please don't go alone to check things out."

When she pulled away, I said, "I didn't go alone. Caroline went with me, but she disappeared when that other ghost showed up." I was glad when nobody asked who Caroline was.

Elsie handed me a glass of her spiked lemonade. "Sounds like you need this more than me."

I took the glass and downed it. "This is so good, Elsie. I'm so sorry everything happened the way it has. Hopefully, the FBI will be able to return your money."

"I hope so, too. Jack really needs to get into the good graces of his son again."

I drank in silence, enjoying the company, but when I asked Sara where Andrew was, she told me he had gone back to the Tawas Beach Resort to gather his belongings. I was glad that he'd be back soon because I really didn't want to be alone tonight, not after everything I've gone through today.

CHAPTER FIFTEEN

I made my way back to the drawing room and Caroline was admiring the picture I had found.

"Who is that?" I asked as she took my hand. In the blink of an eye, I was transported back in time. I now stood in the bedroom where Sheriff Peterson had found the suitcase packed with clothing from the 30s. A very much alive-looking Caroline was packing the suitcase, tears streaming down her cheeks.

When she ran from the room and down the stairs, a man ran after her, brandishing a silver pistol. She screamed as a shot went off, wood splintering on the doorway as she sprinted from the mansion. Caroline ran toward the woods as a man shouted, "Caroline, come back. That woman meant nothing."

Branches scratched Caroline's arms and she raced through the woods and cemetery, making it into town. She panted to regain her breath and strength and stumbled across US 23 just as a black car raced toward her. Agnes could see the man's tense face, his foot slamming on the accelerator, striking Caroline. She flew into the air like a ragdoll, landing with a loud thump in the middle of the street as the car raced away and out of sight.

I knew in an instant that it was the same man whose picture was in the suitcase. He'd murdered Caroline.

I nearly fainted as I fell back into a chair in the drawing room, now transported back to the present. Caroline's ghostly figure was here, too, and so was the man who had murdered her—the same man from the picture.

"I'm so sorry, Caroline," he said. "I didn't mean to run you down, but I just couldn't bear you leaving me."

Caroline's face dropped. Her eyes grew heavy, her teeth bared as she raced toward the man. She shoved him through the door, chasing after him and both of them disappeared. I had to cover my ears now as her screams and wails became louder and louder.

When Sara walked to join me, she didn't seem to see or hear Caroline throwing the man's ghost through one wall after the next.

Caroline picked up the picture. "Where did you get a picture of my grandfather, Malcolm? He really had a tragic life. His fiancé, Caroline, was a victim of a hit and run. He married my grandmother a few years later, but even though she had just given birth to my father, it continued to haunt him enough that he took his own life at the age of thirty-two, right here in the mansion. Right here in the third floor room. I wanted to tell you earlier, but it's just so morbid to talk about that. I suppose after everything you've been through, you deserve to know the truth."

"Thanks, that really explains things. Now I have a clearer understanding about who might haunt the mansion, and who has been haunting me personally." I told her about Caroline, making her promise not to breathe a word to anyone and she readily agreed.

By the time Andrew got to the mansion, things had calmed down. Caroline had quit screaming and her intended, Malcolm, was long gone—at least for the moment.

Andrew took me into his arms and we retreated upstairs. He never asked what had happened and I wasn't willing to tell him the whole truth. Elsie, Mr. Wilson, Bernice, and Millicent were all assigned rooms, and believe me, nobody bothered to ask questions about what had happened, which I was happy about. Even Eleanor, who knew me best, retired to her own room.

I now knew what had really happened to Caroline and why. What was most unclear to me was why she was still here. Perhaps she had stayed to settle the score with Malcolm, but how could she, really? It was clear that Malcolm was a victim of his own jealousy and rage. In one moment, he ran down Caroline and put a whole chain of events into motion. In some way, he must have loved her. Otherwise, why would he agonize so over her death? In a way, Caroline haunted him even though she hadn't been able to come to the mansion until I came here. That wouldn't lessen what he had done, but it explained it to me. Hopefully, in time, they'd settle their differences.

EPILOGUE

"So there's no connection to Barbara Billings' brother Robert and her illegal activities?" I asked Stuart.

"None that we can find. They won't be charged for anything since we were able to recover the money."

"I suppose there's no crime against them lying to me," Sara said as she put a straw to her lips, making sucking sounds as she drank her pink drink with a little umbrella stuck inside.

Stuart nodded. "Background checks is all I can say."

"But I did check. Her Facebook profile seemed on the up and up."

"Yes, but so did the International Energy company that she was selling bogus stock of. It's not worth mentioning since it's non-existent, or a figment of Katherine's imagination," Stuart explained.

"I know. I checked Katherine's page, too. That's how I figured out who Len McGroovy really was—Peyton Murphy. I had no idea that Stuart had been investigating the same man who was involved with Katherine in her scheme, but it seems that Katherine had indeed screwed over the wrong man when she didn't hand any of that cash over to Len. We'll never really know what Katherine had seen that day on the third floor that resulted in her death though. Is that the only reason you came to town, Stuart?"

He squeezed my hand. "Yes and no. When I heard about your accident, I came, didn't I?"

"Yes, but why have you stayed away so long?"

"After college, I went right into the FBI academy. I've always wanted to be a special agent."

"Yes," my daughter Martha agreed. "Always playing cops and robbers." She whispered to me, "He always made me be the criminal."

"I can see that. I hope that both of you have decided not to stay so far away. I'm not getting any younger, you know."

"I can't make any promises, Mother, but I'll try my best."

I left it at that. I had no choice but to take things as they came. Stuart had the right to live his life as he saw fit. It really bothered me to think that he'd put his life in danger as an agent, but in so many ways he was just like his father, my late husband, Tom. Both of them felt inclined to enforce the law.

Eleanor and Andrew joined us on the patio of the Butler Mansion. There hasn't been a vacancy since the mansion opened as a bed and breakfast, and Sara had left it up to Eleanor and me to run the place. One of our first duties was to seal up the third floor room since the ghosts preferred it that way. We were sure to fix the brick wall in that room with all the original bricks as opposed to replacing them with new ones. I'd hate to renovate the place and have the ghosts leave. The truth was that mansion was their home, and home they should stay.

Elsie and Jack were sitting at another table. They had gotten their money back and were quite sweet on one another. I personally couldn't understand it, but as Eleanor had often said, "There was someone for everyone."

Sheriff Peterson and Trooper Sales were enjoying the party as well. I imagined that Peterson was just happy that I had stayed out of his hair on this case for the most part, and I was, too. While they had been involved in the case in some way, the FBI had taken over and wrapped things up.

Caroline has never left my side completely, but she fades in and out at will. As it turns out Caroline is quite useful at times and is always willing to help out, even though Eleanor isn't completely at ease with her presence. All I know is that life has taken a strange turn for all of us and we'd be fools not to accept any extra help that came our way, even if it came from a ghostly apparition. Caroline was here to stay and I was happy to have her as my newest partner in crime.

Thanks to my many readers who have followed the series — you are my constant cheerleaders. Feel free to contact me on Facebook, Facebook, Twitter, or join my email newsletter located on my website http://madisonjohns.com.

ABOUT THE AUTHOR

At forty-four, sleep deprived from a third shift job but certain her years of caring for senior citizens could result in something quite unique, Madison Johns made the decision to write. Little did she realize how her decision was soon to change her life.

Her Agnes Barton Senior Sleuths mystery series not only opened the door to an amazing writing career but also quickly made their way onto Amazon's bestsellers list for cozy mystery and humor. But Agnes and her fellow sleuths didn't stop there. Madison's charming cast of senior characters also went on to three times seize coveted spots on the bestsellers list of USA Today.

With her stories accomplishing feats she had never quite imagined, Madison is now able to live the life she loves—as a full-time writer. When not writing, she spends her days with her two children, a black lab named Sparky, and Jackson, a hilarious Jackson Chameleon who keeps her company while she plots her next series.

Madison is an active participant on Facebook. She loves to hear from readers and fans. Visit her on the web at: http://madisonJohns.com and be sure to follow her on Facebook at www.facebook.com/madisonjohns and http://www.facebook.com/madisonjohnsparanormalromance to keep up with her exciting new Clan of the Werebear paranormal romance series.

Also by this Author

Agnes Barton Senior Sleuths Mystery series in order
Armed and Outrageous
Grannies, Guns and Ghosts
Senior Snoops
Trouble in Tawas
Treasure in Tawas
Bigfoot in Tawas

Box Sets
An Agnes Barton Senior Sleuth Mysteries Box Set (Books 1-3)
An Agnes Barton In Tawas Box Set (Books 4-6)_

Agnes Barton/Kimberly Steele Cozy Mystery series:
Pretty, Hip & Dead

A Cajun Cooking Mystery
Target of Death

Sweet Romance
Pretty and Pregnant (Kimberly Steele Novella)
Redneck Romance(Kelly Gray Standalone)

Paranormal Romance
Hidden, Clan of the Werebear Serial (Book 1)
Discovered, Clan of the Werebear Serial (Book 2)
Betrayed, Clan of the Werebear Serial (Book 3

Made in the USA
Las Vegas, NV
30 April 2022

48175952R00096